AUSTRALIA'S
MAVERICK
MILLIONAIRE

AUSTRALIA'S MAVERICK MILLIONAIRE

BY

MARGARET WAY

MILLS
BOON®

First published in Great Britain 2011
by Mills & Boon, an imprint of Harlequin (UK) Limited.
Large Print edition 2011
Harlequin (UK) Limited, Eton House,
18-24 Paradise Road, Richmond, Surrey TW9 1SR

© Margaret Way, Pty., Ltd 2011

ISBN: 978 0 263 22252 4

Harlequin (UK) policy is to use papers that are natural,
renewable and recyclable products and made from
wood grown in sustainable forests. The logging and
manufacturing process conform to the legal environmental
regulations of the country of origin.

Printed and bound in Great Britain
by CPI Antony Rowe, Chippenham, Wiltshire

PROLOGUE

Now

CLIO was having the dream that had haunted her for years. One half of her was held prisoner by it; the other half was struggling to break free. Eventually she awoke in a sweat, her legs bound by the tangle of bedclothes. She kicked the top sheet away, rolled onto her back, trying to ease her breathing. Her heart was beating so hard and fast it was making her ears pound. Fourteen years since her little cousin Ella, strapped into her stroller, had plunged headlong into Paradise Lagoon but it might have been yesterday her memories were so vivid. Everyone had back alleys in their subconscious: hers had stored away the near tragedy, so it could rerun it at frequent intervals. Sometimes she thought her memories would never recede into shadow—the breathless terror of that day, the sheer disbelief that such a thing could happen, most of all the paralysing panic. Aunt Lisa, now mother of three bright and beautiful teenagers, including Ella, of course, still had her dark moments of recrimination and guilt. She often said she would never forgive herself for her momentary lapse when she'd forgotten to apply the brake to baby Ella's stroller.

It would have been a life-shattering disaster if it hadn't been for Josh Hart, the bad boy of the town, who paradoxically had looked like a golden-haired archangel. Josh Hart had a tragic history that had caused many compassionate souls to turn a blind eye to his many misdemeanours, which had been pretty well a daily occurrence. His mother from all accounts had died of a drug overdose when he was five. His father's identity was unknown.

Joshua had been taken into care, eventually becoming a foster-child who had been shunted from one home to another, arriving in the town less than a year before the Ella incident to live with a distant relative of his mother's, a kindly widow of sixty who'd had little chance of controlling him and had eventually given up. Josh had run wild for much of the time; shoplifting anything that took his eye, flouting authority at every turn, taking joy rides in fancy cars—there wasn't a thing he didn't seem to know about motors or locks—yet amazingly had never damaged let alone crashed said cars. Once he'd taken a high-powered speedboat from the marina in Moon Bay, returning it after a thirty-minute spin. In between times he'd managed a couple of days a week at school, smarter than all the rest of the kids put together. Only if there were defining moments in life when one showed what one was really made of, Josh Hart at age thirteen had shown it that day. Displaying remarkable bravery, he had saved Ella's life without a single thought for his own safety.

Even then he had thrilled and frightened Clio. Nothing had changed.

He still thrilled and frightened her. Only these days he was an admired and respected entrepreneur with a law degree, first-class honours, hanging on his office wall, courtesy of her own grandfather who had made it all possible.

Then

The day had begun brilliantly. It had been the start of the long Christmas vacation and the tropical North had been on the verge of the Wet. *Troppo time*, as it was known, but the arrival of the monsoon had also coincided with a prodigal paradise. Nature had shown itself at its most glorious and extravagant best. The vast tropical landscape had budded, swelled then burst into flamboyant flower accompanied by scents so sweet and aromatic they had filled the immediate world. The great crimson arches of the poincianas had lent welcome shade while colouring the air. The tulip trees had broken out their lovely orange cups, and the cassias had spilled yellow blossom in a wide circle beneath them. It was like being caught in a spell.

It was Aunt Lisa who decided they would go on a picnic. "What do you think, Paradise Lagoon?"

Where else?

Aunt Lisa had chosen the town's most beautiful cool haven, a lush, park-like reserve dominated by a deep emerald lake with its gorgeous mantle of a thousand tropical waterlilies, all blue and all planted by her family, recognized experts on waterlilies and all manner of tropical plants. There was the Whitaker with its gigantic lavender blue blossoms and bright yellow stamens; the Trickett, a Campanula blue and her dead grandmother's favourite; the star-shaped Astraea that held its lovely head so high above the water the flowers could be seen from quite a distance. Even the low stone wall topped by tall wrought-iron railings was a living glory with bridal white bougainvillea in foaming extravagance vying with the lagoon's glorious lilies.

They set off happily in Aunt Lisa's car, feeling not a shadow of concern, when one of the town's characters, named Snowy, and quite a drinker, claimed to have spotted a "saltie" at the far end of the lagoon a few weeks back.

"Watch out for that fella now," Snowy had warned in the pub, brandishing his schooner aloft. "Plenty big enough. Round six metres, I reckon."

That had raised a few laughs. Most people thought what Snowy had seen was a thick forward floating log, although his claim was checked out as a matter of course. This was crocodile country after all. Anywhere north of the Tropic of Capricorn was.

People lived with their crocodiles. The trick was never to venture into a crocodile's territory. Australia's salt-water crocodile was one of the largest reptiles in the world. Crocs would take anything that strayed too near the water—humans, cattle, even big buffaloes, horses, dogs; anything in the water, turtles being a delicacy. Only a crocodile had never been sighted in Paradise Lagoon for more than a decade. Back then a young Japanese tourist who'd had far too much to drink had decided on a midnight swim despite the warning signs in several languages, including Japanese, and his equally intoxicated mate shouting at him not to be a fool. The mate had got it right. A crocodile had been lying in wait for just such a heaven-sent opportunity. It had snaffled up the hapless young man, subjecting him to the death roll before stashing him away at the bottom of the lagoon until such time as it was ready to feast.

That tragic event had horrified the town. The crocodile, although a protected species, had been shot dead and the lagoon trawled in case it had had a mate. No mate had been found. The town breathed a huge collective sigh of relief. Everyone knew the Wet was breeding time. The female crocodile, much smaller than the male, laid her eggs, some 40 to 60, along the banks of rivers, billabongs and lagoons. No human or animal had been taken in the intervening years and no nests spotted anywhere amid the density of the aquatic reeds and grasses. Still, there was perpetual vigilance. Crocs had been known to come with surprising speed across land in search of more congenial lagoons.

The town loved its parkland but no one *swam* in the lagoon. That was strictly forbidden. No local was that much of a fool anyway. Most people had swimming pools. Paradise Lagoon was a favourite picnicking spot. There was a special playground for the little ones and excellent bar-beque areas with dining rotundas adjacent for family occasions. Bicycle paths. Walking paths. Children under the age of twelve who entered the parkland had to be under the supervision of an adult, though the danger of going near the water was drummed into children as toddlers. Even little kids heeded the message. Crocodiles were not friendly. Crocodiles ate people.

Not a problem for them. They were with Aunt Lisa. So there was Lisa, baby Ella, herself and her best friend, Tulip, both of them nine years old, in the same class at school. Up until that day she had enjoyed an idyllic childhood, the privileged and adored only child of Lyle and Allegra Templeton. The Templetons were the richest family in the entire North. Her grand-father, Leo Templeton, had as a young man in-herited a pastoral fortune worth millions. Leo's father and his father before him had built up the Templeton fortune with sheep and cattle; Leo Templeton had taken it to new heights as a result of his own Midas touch and clever diversifica-tion. The family now controlled multiple enterprises, all of them highly successful. Her parents were the town's most popular young couple. She, as her grandfather always claimed, was the jewel in the Templeton crown.

"Not a girl alive who can touch you!"

Of course he was biased in the extreme. But she *was* liked by everyone and she felt she would have been even if her name hadn't been Templeton.

They picnicked on the delicious food Aunt Lisa had packed into her state-of-the-art picnic basket—little chicken and mushroom pies, scotch eggs, ham quiche or sandwiches, washed down with cold sparkling apple juice followed by some lovely, fudgy brownies if they had room. They did. Baby Ella, eighteen months old, sat happily in her stroller, staring adoringly at her mother with her radiant blue eyes. Afterwards Clio and Tulip lay back on the grass, eyes closed, talking about all the things nine year old girls talked about—school friends, movies, pop idols, the new bike Tulip had graduated to, her ballet lessons. Aunt Lisa casually read a book, Ella gurgled her pleasure in the beautiful day.

Before they returned home they took a leisurely

walk around the park, admiring the brilliantly plumaged parrots and lorikeets that thronged the trees. At one point Aunt Lisa's mobile rang. She and Tulip continued on walking while Aunt Lisa turned away to answer her phone.

That's when it happened.

The stroller with a plump, wriggling toddler in it moved slowly but very worryingly off the path. Without its brake applied, it began a slow downward slide over the grass, picking up speed so its progress eventually turned into a freewheeling hurtle. A tree or a shrub might have stopped its progress, but there were none in the way. The slope was not significant yet the stroller with Ella in it was taking a dead straight path to the water, covering the not-inconsiderable distance to the lagoon in heart-shaking seconds, before plunging into the deep emerald depths and disappearing out of sight.

Aunt Lisa, turning back in alarm, dropped her mobile, screaming her unspeakable terror. Some residents said afterwards they heard her screams half a mile away. Tulip, heart in her mouth, fainted, her slight body swooping to the grass. Clio stood paralysed, knowing when her limbs unlocked she would have to take a header into the lagoon to save Ella. She was a good swimmer, but like everyone else she had never ventured into the lagoon, said to be fathomless at the centre. But this was a life-and-death situation.

She gathered herself, mumbling a prayer, only at that precise moment, out of nowhere, a tall, athletic boy with a thick shock of hair that glinted gold in the sun suddenly materialized. He was moving as fleetly as a young lion loping down the grassy slope before diving so cleanly into the lagoon scarcely a ripple broke the surface.

People were charging across the reserve now, not quite knowing what was happening but ready to offer any help that was needed. No one was ever free of the fear of crocodiles. Everyone knew Aunt Lisa. She was a Templeton after all. Everyone knew about adorable Baby Ella. But where *was* Ella? They had the answer in moments. A roar of relief split the air as Josh's golden head, dripping water and green gunk, broke the glassy surface. He had one arm firmly wrapped around Ella.

Thank you, thank you, thank you, God. Thank you, thank you, thank you, Josh.

It was her turn now to race down the slope. She was fully prepared to dive in to help Josh, only he shouted at her fiercely to stay back that mortified tears sprang to her eyes.

A woman, an off-duty nurse, took charge of Ella, checking her before putting her into her frantic mother's arms. Next the nurse attended to Tulip, who had come round. She was sitting up, but was ghastly pale. Two strong men were on hand to pull Joshua out of the water, though his expression registered he was fully capable of getting out himself. That was the moment an elderly woman screamed and they all became aware a terrible weapon of destruction was coming at speed from the far end of the lagoon, its infamous notches of eyes and nostrils just visible above the waterline. The crocodile was nowhere as big as Snowy had claimed, probably a female, but it could have taken boy and little girl with no trouble at all.

Josh Hart fell back panting onto the grass, golden arms and legs spread-eagled. She had never in her life spoken more than two words to him but Clio found herself dropping onto the grass beside him. "Did you know the croc was there?" she asked, not daring to touch his tanned, outflung arm.

His fine nostrils flared. "Don't be stupid, little girl." He turned his golden-blond head to stare at her, blue eyes ablaze. "There are always crocs around. Snowy did *warn* you complacent idiots," he added, adult-like scathing judgement plain on his beautiful, utterly superior face. He might try all he liked to be wicked. She knew he would never pull it off with her.

"But the council men checked," she offered in protest. *When* had they checked?

"Well, they got it wrong, didn't they?" His brilliant eyes burned into her.

"It's my little cousin, Ella, you saved."

"I *know*." His answer was short and dismissive.

She flushed at the hostility he gave off in waves. Did he hate her?

"You're Clio Templeton, aren't you?" he said

unexpectedly. "The town's little sweetheart, its princess."

His sarcastic tone was no proof against her eternal gratitude. "And you're a *hero*," she said simply. Then, greatly daring, she bent to kiss his cheek. "I'll never forget what you did today, Josh Hart."

A look of intense wariness and some other emotion she couldn't quite catch came into his dazzling blue eyes. "Yes, you will."

"Never!" She stood up, nine years old, long slender legs, tall for her age, her gleaming sable hair cascading down her back, admiration in her huge dark eyes. "I know a lot of things they say about you are true, Josh Hart, but you're *brave*. I'm proud to know you."

He laughed, such a strange laugh. "Hush now, princess," he said, and one-armed himself to his feet. "They're calling for you."

Afterwards Clio felt as though lightning had been crackling all around them.

She was destined to feel it every time she laid eyes on him.

CHAPTER ONE

WHEN did falling in love begin? Josh pondered as he drove through the starry night.

When one was thirteen years old and a beautiful little girl with long gypsy dark hair and huge lustrous dark eyes bent down to kiss his cheek? When he'd had to swallow painfully hard against a great welling spring of barely remembered emotion? When he'd caught a dazzling glimpse of happiness, a meaning, and a purpose in life? No one outside his tragic mother had ever kissed him or moved his heart. But Clio Templeton had pulled him out of his deep emotional void that unforgettable day. In a way it had transformed him. Made up for a lot of the deprivation he had suffered. Only nine years old but little Clio Templeton had penetrated a shield so thick and strong he had thought no one could get through it. That was until she'd put her rosebud mouth very gently to his water-slicked cheek.

Clio Templeton, the only person in the world to make a breakthrough in the harrowing years since his mother had left him. He didn't believe to this day his mother had overdosed deliberately. She had loved him. And he had loved her. They had been two against the world. He had no idea who his father was, a callous man at any rate. Maybe he could go the same way. He had to *physically* resemble the man who had fathered him, because his mother, Carol, had been dark haired, hazel eyed and petite of stature. Whoever his biological father had been, his mother had never revealed his name. And this was the man who had destroyed her dreams, then her life, leaving him a desolate orphan.

So that was his history. His mother had died. He had been left alive with all chance of normal life slipped away. He had been left to cope with life from age five. Total incomprehension. Grief. Loneliness. Extreme isolation. They had even renamed him, picking someone from the Bible. His given name had sounded too foreign. With the years came the terrible anger. He had seethed with it. Not burying it deep. It had all been there on show. As he had grown, his body had become solid muscle. He had eventually shot up to six-three. A formidable height. A formidable body. Back then he might have been a young lion escaped from the zoo. So that was God's great plan for him, was it? he had reasoned. A probable life in prison? He no longer believed in a God. Why would he? Shunted from one home to another, juvenile detention, he had seen it all, some of it much too shocking to speak of.

He'd had to rise above his past, every rotten episode. But the monumental effort had made him depressingly hard, separating him from other people. No chinks in his armour. He knew a lot of the good people in the town backed off him. They didn't have the understanding to realize what he'd been through. Probably wouldn't believe it anyway. They after all had led charmed lives. The tropical town of Templeton was as physically beautiful and prosperous as anywhere in the Promised Land.

* * *

By the time he arrived at the Templeton mansion, the cul-de-sac that fronted the estate and the sweeping driveway was parked with luxury cars, the most expensive of them all belonging to Jimmy Crowley. Hell, Crowley was only a year older than he was. The car would have suited rich Granddaddy Crowley better, the old scoundrel, raw, ugly, powerful, but Jimmy was struggling to get across that he too could also become a man of substance. He had to be because Jimmy, along with his family, had convinced themselves Clio Templeton was Jimmy's. Who else *could* it be but the most beautiful girl in the world? God knew, Josh didn't disagree with that.

When he climbed out of his metallic grey Porsche, the scented summer air wrapped around him—frangipani, oleander, gardenia, the rich white ginger blossom and the king jasmine. He found himself gasping with the sheer pleasure of taking in the mingled fragrances. Just about every beautiful tropical flower and plant was represented in the gardens. There was no shortage of space. The Templeton mansion occupied twenty acres of prime real estate even the

Templetons would be hard pressed to buy these days. The splendour of the gardens was known state wide. They were opened to the public from time to time. Leo's mother had had constructed a huge eight-acre manmade fresh-water lake—no crocs to cause concern—with an amazing waterfall spilling over extraordinary big boulders that had been found in the area or brought in. The water supply came from a dam sited well away from the house. No one looking at the lake would ever know it was artificial. The verges were surrounded by luxuriant natural grasses and bullrushes, huge stands of the pure white arum lily, Japanese water iris and groves of tree ferns. The lake was a focal point for the magnificent grounds.

He looked towards the house. The scale of the place over the years had become little short of heroic. There was a certain absurdity to that, seeing that these days only two people, Leo and his granddaughter, lived there. Leo's wife, Margaret, had died ten or more years back. The long-time housekeeper, Meg Palmer, and her husband, Tom, Leo's man Friday, had their own very comfortable and private bungalow in the grounds.

The mansion lit up was a sight to take the breath away—vast, white, tropical colonial style with touches of South East Asia that were evident in the fine timber fretwork that was featured throughout the grand residence. The festive season was coming on. Leo liked to entertain. In no time it would be Christmas, with the Templeton big annual Christmas Eve party, not that Christmas meant anything to Josh. He had no one. There had been women in his life, of course. Sex eased many tensions but real emotion evaded him. There was no woman he had wanted to allow into his daily life; no one could thaw his heart or navigate his quiet but perilous moods. Sometimes he thought he had no choice but to remain forever a loner. He knew it could happen.

One hundred of the town's richest and most influential citizens had been invited to tonight's party. It was to raise more funds for neonatal equipment, which didn't come cheap. The Templetons had actually put up most of the money for the town's highly accredited hospital. Guests were naturally expected to plunge their hands deep into their pockets. The usual sumptuous buffet would be provided. Leo had insisted he come, though he would have refused had it been anyone else, with the only exception the exquisite Clio.

Not that Clio would have invited him. He and Clio were to stay a safe distance from one another. He had got the message early. Clio was the princess. He was the pauper. Consequently they had not been allowed to grow in any way closer, though he often saw her when he visited Leo. His visits were not so frequent these days. He had reached the point early in life when he was already a millionaire a satisfying number of times over. These days he was *the* property man. Real estate made fortunes more than anything else short of mining and he had interests in that. The North had been enjoying a tremendous building boom. He had made the most of it, buying up broken-down properties, putting up lucrative apartments, office blocks and a new shopping mall.

Leo had financed him at the beginning. He had paid Leo back with interest. Leo Templeton had made a better life possible for him. He was acutely aware how much he owed Leo, who had stepped in after the "baby Ella" incident to take on a trusteeship, a milder form of guardianship, of him. But Leo's granddaughter was too rare a creature to be tainted by *his* squalid past. Whatever residual feeling remained from that day years ago, both hid it so deep it might never be allowed to surface.

Clio had lived with her grandfather since Lyle Templeton, Clio's father, had remarried a few years back. Clio's mother had been killed in a yachting catastrophe when two yachts had collided at sea. Clio had been seventeen at the time, devastated by her loss and the bizarre way it had happened. They had been as close as mother and daughter could be.

There was no rapport whatever with the second Mrs. Templeton. Keeley Templeton was many years younger than Lyle, no great beauty like Clio's mother Allegra, with her aristocratic Italian background, but she had turned herself into a glamour girl with an endless flow of small talk that was good for such functions.

Inside the mansion, the entrance hall, big enough to park several cars, was filled with people who had gone through the receiving formalities and were making their way into the reception rooms. Josh was one of the last to arrive, just as he planned. Leo, still a fine, handsome man but looking frailer every time he saw him, was standing with his beautiful granddaughter, receiving their guests as they arrived. How easy it was to see Clio had been born to wealth and privilege and a mix of only the best genes. Her mother had been a member of a patrician Florentine family.

Lyle Templeton had met Allegra when he had been visiting Italy as part of his Grand Tour. Their meeting place, the iconic Uffizi, where both of them had been contemplating Botticelli's "The Birth of Venus". Allegra at that time had been a very promising art student and a highly cultured young woman. She had spoken English. He'd had no Italian but they had fallen madly in love. On sight. The classic *coup de foudre*. Scarred as he was within, Josh *knew* that could happen. The sight of Clio Templeton even as a nine-year-old was graven into his mind.

"Good to see you, Josh!" Leo beamed as the two men shook hands. Leo's pleasure was so obvious that quite a few people stopped in the middle of their conversations to wonder why the patrician Leo Templeton had taken this tall, stunningly handsome but definitely edgy young man under his wing. He might have been a gatecrasher such was their disapproval, albeit carefully hidden. No one dared to put that disapproval on plain view. No one wished to offend Leo, of course. No one wanted to offend the likes of Josh Hart.

Now they were facing each other. "Good evening, Josh." Clio addressed him in her charming voice.

"How are you, Clio?" His eyes consumed her. That was the best part of his blue eyes. They burned, or so he'd been told, but they gave away no hint of his inner emotions. That's what made him a brilliant poker player.

"I'm very well, thank you." She tilted her lovely oval face up to him.

She had beautifully marked eyebrows, her dark eyes huge. She looked exquisite, the ideal model for a fine painting. He had learned from Leo that her mother had called her Clio after the subject of one of Allegra's favourite paintings, Vermeer's *The Allegory of Painting* depicting the Muse of History, Clio. With that in mind he had actually taken a side trip from Rome to Vienna to check out the painting in the museum where it was held. All in all he had spent a lot of time in art museums at home and abroad. He had made it his business to educate himself way beyond his Law-Commerce Degree, which Leo had made possible, cramming so much into a few short years, vast amounts of learning and knowledge. It amused him that he was something of a natural scholar. But the beautiful Clio was to be no part of his life. He was excluded from the Templeton ranks.

Tonight she was wearing a long satin dress in a colour that beggared description. It was neither green nor gold but a blend of the two. The plaited straps that held the bodice were knotted over her collarbone. There was another knot beneath the discreetly plunging neckline; a wide black sash showed off her narrow waist. Her wonderful sable hair was arranged with the classic centre parting and drawn back from her honey-skinned face into intricate loops. Three-tiered pendant earrings swung from her ears. He thought the stones were citrine, mandarin garnet and amethyst, probably Bulgari. She looked ravishing, a sheen all over her.

Did the excitement in her presence ever go away? He wanted no other woman but her. The one woman he couldn't have.

He had only just moved from the receiving line into the living room that was so richly and elegantly furnished it could have featured in *Architectural Digest* when Keeley Templeton broke away from her group to come towards him with a show of enthusiasm that put him right on edge.

"Josh!" Her smile held the usual sexual come-on. "This *is* a surprise!" She laughed, going so far as to attempt to draw him into a hug, only he took her hand, holding it down firmly to her side.

"I don't think so, Keeley." There was a warning grate in his voice. "Your husband is over there. He mightn't like it."

"Probably not," she sighed. "But you do look *wonderful*, Josh. I've never seen a man look better in a dinner jacket. Terrific line and cut, and I especially love white dinner jackets in the summer."

"And you look quite exceptionally dolled up," he remarked very dryly, his eyes a startlingly blue in the golden tan of his face.

"Don't you like it?" She looked down at herself, then made a little face. She was wearing a short, strapless red dress sewn with crystals all over the bodice. It had cost the earth, and it showed off her legs, which were good. "Why don't you come join us?" she invited, glancing back to where her husband and a group of friends were in conversation. "You must want a drink."

Josh looked over her bright chestnut head with its fashionable blonde streaks, taking note of the people in the room. Many an overt stare shifted immediately when he focused on them. He knew he had a jittery effect on a lot of people. "Why is that?" he asked. "Why must I want a drink?"

Keeley gave a playful moan. Josh Hart fascinated her. She knew for a fact he fascinated every woman in town. The guy was drop-dead sexy and incredibly handsome, though strange to say he appeared uncaring about it. "I guess that's what I love about you, Josh." She knew her near-uncontrollable lust for him was leaving her wide open to trouble. "You're so difficult."

"You're sure you don't mean I don't play games, Keeley?" He was getting ready to walk away from her. He knew Keeley was attracted to him. Big time. She wasn't doing terribly well at hiding it. He knew perfectly well people had affairs in the town; quite a few here tonight, even standing in the same group as if they were all good pals. The hypocrisy of it all! Keeley was *married*, and to Clio's father, who was a fine-looking man, if a real snob. That alone should have given her pause and made her behave. Probably she'd already had a drink or two. Lyle Templeton was, in fact, watching their exchange with an eagled-eyed intensity just short of a glare, his tanned cheeks turning red at what could have been construed as a public humiliation.

"God, I wish you would," Keeley leaned closer towards him, helpless beneath the force of attraction he exuded.

"Unless you want me to stomp hard on your pretty toes, you'd better walk away, Keeley," he warned. No use playing the gentleman with Keeley. "I definitely don't want trouble."

"As if you couldn't handle it!" She gave him a conspiratorial wink, a little unsteady on her expensive red and black stilettos.

Reluctantly he put a steadying hand to her elbow. "Walk away *now*, Keeley."

"Why, when I find it so much more exciting talking to you? Why don't you like me, Josh?" she crooned, her expression utterly exposed. "Is it because people are watching?"

"Don't be such a fool," he bit out, the muscles along his sculpted jaw clenching. This wasn't a staged performance. Keeley really did find him thrilling, God help her.

* * *

Across the room Clio saw Josh's blue eyes start to smoulder and burn. She knew he had long since learned how to withhold any powerful bouts of anger but she could see he was turning edgy. It was there in his frozen stance, the rigid set of his chiselled jaw. She was something of an expert on Josh's body language. Even the squaring of his wide shoulders was ominous. Keeley was being sickeningly indiscreet, making a fool of her father. Soon *everyone* would know how infatuated she was with Josh. That presented a whole raft of complications. The attraction concerned her greatly, though she understood Josh's magnetic pull. With Keeley's short scarlet dress and her palpable air of excitement, she gave the impression she was about to explode.

Since Keeley had married her father she had started to dress up to the nines. In some ways she had become a different person, assuming a softer, more polished appearance. Clio realized with a shiver of apprehension there was the potential for disaster here. Keeley was two people. The first, her father's wife; the other, a woman, Clio suspected, who had a largely unfulfilled sexual appetite. And that appetite was for Josh.

Keeley had chosen her father for his money and the position it afforded her. The marriage wasn't working out. Should anyone be surprised? Only Clio and her grandfather knew Keeley had claimed to have fallen pregnant before the marriage. Unintentionally, of course. Her grandfather had urged a DNA test, proving paternity. Her father wanted no part of that. The child was his. He would take full responsibility. Only the child turned out to be either a secret miscarriage or a phantom pregnancy. Keeley Bradley had been no inexperienced young woman. She had been in her late twenties at the time of the marriage, a trail of lovers behind her.

After her mother had drowned, her father, hitherto so happy, had turned into a sad, solitary man, who would forever mourn the loss of his wife. He had broken down at the funeral, sobbing out his wish to have drowned with her. But here had been a man of forty-five, in the prime of life. After a decent period of time, he had been advised by everyone who cared for him to try to move on. Allegra was gone. He had the rest of his life to live out. His response?

"Move on? I don't know what that means, Clio. I'm lost in limbo with little hope of getting out."

Much as her father loved her, Clio knew she was no replacement for her mother.

No one was.

Ironically Keeley Bradley had entered their lives at her father's 50th birthday party, given by Leo for a small group of family and close friends. Keeley had gained entry by virtue of partnering Clio's playboy cousin, Peter, when his previous date had had to cancel with a migraine. Keeley was a very provocative young woman and she had looked on serious wealth for the first time. She had gone after Lyle with the full force of her sexuality. Her father in the end was only human. Women could and did use sex as a weapon. Keeley had brought her father down.

Her movements so flowing they hid all sense of urgency, Clio skirted various groups with a smile and a few words, arriving at Josh's side within seconds. She placed her hand on the sleeve of his white dinner jacket, feeling the hard musculature beneath the cloth. "Excuse me, won't you?" She glanced at her stepmother, who stared back at her with a battery of expressions, dislike predominating. "I wonder if I could speak to you for a moment, Josh?"

He felt a certain degree of contempt for himself as sensations crashed around inside his chest. She had only put her hand on his arm yet it had much the same effect as a charge of electricity. Apart from the kiss on his cheek he had received from her a lifetime ago, this was the first time she had actually touched him, albeit through his dinner jacket.

You're one pathetic guy!

Yet his response couldn't have emerged from a smoother or more in-control mouth. "Why, of course." He knew Clio did everything graciously, but he saw her sudden appearance for what it was. Diplomatic intervention. Clio had the art of creating a serene atmosphere in her grandfather's mansion. And she was nobody's fool. She had very accurately deduced how he was feeling, how her stepmother was looking for a bit of dangerous sex on the side. Apparently he qualified. It was Clio's job to keep watch.

She led him through one of the sets of doors into the cooling, star-studded night. The French doors opened out onto a wide covered verandah with a polished teak floor. Beyond that, the broad floodlit terrace with acres and acres of magnificent tropical gardens before them were also illuminated. The rhythmic splash of the waterfall into the lake carried clearly on the night air. A caressing breeze blew, bringing with it the intoxicating scent of gardenias. As Clio moved she signalled one of the young uniformed waiters who brought out champagne on a silver tray to them.

"Have one, please, Josh," she said, as far away from him as the stars in the sky. "I don't suppose it's your drink of choice?"

He removed a frosted flute from the tray, passed it to her, felt the shock waves all over again as her fingers fleetingly touched his. "Drink of choice? There's not much I don't like in the way of alcohol, Clio, except maybe rum. Red wine I very much like. Champagne, especially when it's

French, like now," he commented dryly, on the Bollinger. "It's the only white wine I really like. I'm not one of the Chardonnay set."

"Good. Neither am I. So drink it."

"Yes, my lady."

"Don't do that, Josh," she begged. No one could call Josh an *easy* person. He had such an edge.

"Well, you are far, far above me, aren't you?" he said with a faint taunt, thinking he was living proof that a strong man could be held in thrall by a woman.

She gave him a long look out of her lustrous dark eyes. "You've come a long way since you were a boy, Josh. False modesty must sound ridiculous even to yourself. My grandfather thinks the world of you. He gets prouder and prouder every day. You're a big success story, Josh. You're the sort of grandson Leo wanted but never got."

"He got someone far better. He got *you*."

She shrugged her bare shoulders. Her skin was a lovely even honey gold, showing her Italian heritage. "He loves me as I love him. But I'm a *woman*. Men like my grandfather needed sons, grandsons. Leo believes men are unquestionably the natural-born leaders. Sons take over and carry on the family businesses. They build on already amassed fortunes."

"There are plenty of brilliant businesswomen," Josh freely acknowledged. "I've met a few over the last couple of years, as sharp as tacks."

"You're a different breed, Josh," she sighed. "And you're *young*." Josh was only twenty-eight, though he appeared older he had such presence.

"So what are you saying here, Clio? You have issues?"

"Of course I do," she said.

"But you're an associate in Templeton & Company. One day you'll make full partner."

"And be assured of a sizzling career? I don't think so. Much as my grandfather and my father love me, they want to keep me away from all unpleasantness, as if I'm a little girl. I handle the genteel side of business. Wills, conveyancing, minor disputes, that sort of thing."

He knew it was true. "Still, I understand their motivation. In a way. You're very precious to them. Jimmy is not up to the mark?"

"Jimmy tries. He's a very different person from

his father," she said, taking a sip of champagne as though she needed a pause.

"So Vince Crowley is the pick of the bunch? How bright is that? Second rate?"

"You're not an avid fan of the Crowleys?"

He looked intently into her beautiful face. "And *you* are? You'd need at least a category-five cyclone to put wind beneath Jimmy's sails."

"I suppose." She had to laugh.

"And all the Crowleys think Leo's beautiful granddaughter is within reach." His loathing of the very idea momentarily got the better of him.

"Wishful thinking, I'd say. You're taking a quantum leap, aren't you, Josh? Our rules of engagement have hitherto prohibited much in the way of personal remarks."

"*Your* decision, wasn't it?" he answered sardonically.

"Did it seem like that to you?" It hadn't been her decision at all. Her father only a few years back had gone so far as to forbid her to get anywhere near Josh Hart.

He's a very damaged young man. And dangerous. I've read his case file. It was on Dad's desk. Did you know he beat one of his minders to a pulp?

He probably deserved it, she had said at the time.

That hadn't gone down well with her father, who seemed truly fearful of any connection between her and Josh. It was bad enough for her father that Leo had become Josh's mentor. Clio suspected her father, whether he realized it or not, was jealous of Leo's affection and high regard for that problematic young man.

"Well?" she repeated, "did it seem like that to you?"

"Very much so." Josh's eyes seemed fixed on a distance far beyond the present.

"That's how screwed up our lives have been," she sighed.

He stared at her, the master of deadpan, yet he felt consternation underneath. "Am I supposed to make a comment on that?"

"Why not? You're allowed to. Your early life was hard, Josh, I could never know how hard, but these days as a highly successful business-man you've gained a reputation for honesty and integrity. You always were smarter than the rest of us," she added drolly.

"You learn a lot of skills in juvenile detention," he told her very bluntly.

"How to beat someone up?"

His blue eyes were like missiles programmed to make a direct hit. "Now why aren't I shocked? You've been reading my files, Clio."

"No, no!" Rapidly she shook her head. Not that she hadn't wanted to. "That would be a massive infringement of privacy. Leo definitely wouldn't have approved."

"So who was it, your dad? Your father would love me to disappear overnight. Why is that, do you suppose?" he asked, knowing the answer full well.

"General over-protectiveness. Even when you know someone loves you, you don't want them to watch your every move. Dad hated it when I moved out. But I couldn't live with Keeley. I dislike her intensely and the feeling is mutual. As for Dad, he thinks there's a worrying connection between the two of us. A bond that was forged years ago."

"Wasn't it?" he asked, without missing a beat. "I was your hero for a day."

She waited for a moment, not *even* certain what to say. From that day on Josh had found a place in her heart and mind. "What I thought of you hasn't changed, Josh. You cover up what you feel. I cover up what I feel. It's safer that way."

"For whom, exactly?" he asked flatly. "Your family, the entire community. I'm still the bad boy in town. That won't change."

"It won't if you don't let it."

"Get real, Clio!" he scoffed. "Anyway, I'm in no rush to reassure people I don't have any respect for or interest in. Maybe *you* can tell me why Jimmy Crowley always looks like the cat that's got the cream?"

"Sheer bravado!" she said. "Poor Jimmy has grown up terrified of his grandfather and his father."

"At least he shows some smarts. Old Paddy is an out-and-out villain." Josh voiced his contempt. "As for Vince, he's Mr Nice Guy in public— just look at the way he's acting back there in the house. All buffed up, big white smile, dense hair, rocking back on his evening shoes, the extravagant *bonhomie*! I'm certain he's a very different character at home. Susan Crowley with all the forced smiles. Poor woman can't open her mouth without his consent."

"Tell me about it," she said, hesitating a moment. "I haven't spoken to anyone about this, but Susan has approached me to represent her in a divorce action."

Josh snapped to full attention "*What?* How can you do that, Clio? Vince is a full partner in the law firm. You're an associate. Major conflict of interest surely?"

"I'm thinking of going out on my own."

His broad forehead knotted. "You're serious?"

"About time," she said briefly. "I'm only an ornament where I am."

He couldn't argue with that. "And you've discussed this with Leo?" She couldn't have. Everyone in the town knew Leo had his beautiful granddaughter on a pedestal. *Untouchable. Far from harm's way.*

"No." She faced him directly. The exterior lights gilded her flawless skin and added lustre to the fabric of her lovely gown. 'You're the first to know. I'm discussing it with *you* because I trust you, because you've seen so much of life, so much cruelty both hidden and on show, you would know where I'm coming from. I suspect Susan Crowley has endured hell."

"I believe you." Josh jammed his hands in his trouser pockets so he couldn't reach for her. All his feelings for her, deep and romantic as they were, had to be kept under wraps. "What I don't get is she has a son to defend her. What sort of a gutless wonder is he? No one would have hurt my mother with me there."

Clio shook her head. "I'm sure he doesn't physically abuse her."

"You can't know that. But I suppose he's not that stupid," Josh gritted out. "There are all kinds of abuse. Susan Crowley's kind would probably be mental and emotional abuse. Crowley is one of those men who have to have total sway over the women in their lives."

"Exactly."

Josh lowered his resonant voice. "Leo will never agree," he warned her.

"Would that I were a *grandson!*" Clio raised her slender hands, palms up. A gesture of frustration.

"I'm just so happy you're not!" The words sprang from his mouth.

She turned to stare at him out of her lustrous dark eyes. "Do you mean that, Josh, or was that the sort of answer men come up with?"

He shrugged. "Make what you will of it."

"Now, don't get angry with me, Josh." She surrendered to her own sublimated longings. She touched his arm as if in conciliation.

"Please don't equate me with other guys you know, Clio," he said, staring down at her elegant, long-fingered hand. "You're a beautiful, clever woman, a smart, skilful lawyer. *You're* the one with the empty words. You wouldn't *want* to be a man."

"Of course I don't," she admitted, removing her hand. "I'm only pointing out that in my family it would make things so much easier if I were. Both Leo and Dad were against me studying law. An arts degree would have done nicely. It's okay for you, Leo's brilliant protégée. Not all that suitable for Leo's clever granddaughter. It's no secret I don't need to work. I could devote myself to charitable work and good deeds. The only trouble is I want and *need* to use my brain. I need to make my own money, live my own life. Find personal fulfilment."

"You won't find it with Jimmy Crowley."

The heat and energy level between them was rising. To an onlooker, and there were plenty, they were a study in contrasts: Clio, a beautiful young woman with her warm Mediterranean colouring; Josh, the very picture of the classic blue-eyed blond alpha man. "Don't push it, Josh," Clio said. It was her turn to warn him.

"I apologise. You could leave town," he suggested, his blue eyes trained on her.

She threw up her dark head so impetuously her pendant earrings danced, flashing lights across her cheeks. "Do you honestly think I haven't thought about it? I used to all the time. But I can't leave Leo right now. He's been diagnosed with a heart condition. You know about that?"

"I do," Josh confirmed. "Leo has told me about his heart condition. Not serious, he said. As a matter of fact, being Leo, he laughed if off as if he was going to live for ever."

"My mother's life came to an end when she was only forty-one," Clio offered in a soft, melancholy voice. "I'll never come to terms with it. I adored my mother. No one could ever take her place. In that way I'm exactly like Dad."

"At least you had her that long." Josh was battling his own fume of emotions, not the least of it his dangerous desire for a fascinating but unobtainable woman.

She could feel the hot flush that mounted to her cheeks. "I'm sorry, Josh. That was really insensitive. I wasn't thinking for a moment. I know what a rotten time you've had."

"The fact is you *don't*, Clio," he corrected her tersely, "and I'm not about to tell you." They were surrounded by people laughing, talking, light classical music being piped through the house, but they might have been quite alone on a desert island. Josh looked out over the magnificent illuminated tropical gardens. "Your world has been safe. My world was damned scary—sinister might be a better word."

She studied the handsome profile presented to her. He was almost painfully handsome. "You would never dream of sharing your experiences with someone who wanted only to help you?" she asked gently, though she knew it might be folly.

"Are we talking professional help here, Clio?" He swung his gleaming gold head back to her, gazing down his perfectly straight nose. "I had all that. One shrink called me a master manipulator. I think I was about ten at the time. Anyway, let's get off me," he said edgily.

"You don't *want* me to get to know you, Josh?" she dared ask. Was he any different from the boy who had ordered her so harshly to go away?

"Clio, there are things about me I don't wish you to hear. All right?"

Of a sudden she realized that for Josh that might qualify as an appeal. She held up her hands in surrender. "I get the message. Let's get back to me and my world. Dad is desperately unhappy. He should never have married Keeley. They have nothing in common. Not that any woman wouldn't have had a battle as the second Mrs Templeton. So you tell me, Josh. Should I turn my back on my family when they need me and go forge another life for myself maybe thousands of miles away, like Sydney or Melbourne? I have my great-aunts and many contacts there."

"So you're stuck for the time being," he conceded. Leo and her father weren't the only ones who couldn't bear to lose sight and sound of her. "Why doesn't your father divorce Keeley? He must know she only married him for his money."

"Dad doesn't believe in divorce." She felt racked by pity.

"He thinks it's better to live with a woman who doesn't love him?" Josh asked, never in any danger of being attracted to the over-sexed Keeley with the practised throaty laugh. "That's a character flaw he can live with?"

"Apparently," Clio admitted with an effort. "I know I'm risking making you angry again, Josh, but…"

Such a glitter came into his eyes. "Then don't risk it, Clio," he said.

"So you're going to saddle *me* with the worry. You don't want me to say it."

"Are you actually making judgements about *my* moral responses?"

"No, no I'm just thinking about consequences."

"So you've appointed yourself watchdog?"

He looked incredibly superior. Unyielding. No vulnerability there. "I suppose I should apologize."

"You *should*," he said tautly. "Come down off your pedestal, Clio. I wouldn't take up with your stepmother if she were the last woman on earth."

She felt a wash of remorse. "Only Keeley has taken it into her head there's some attraction there."

"Really?" His handsome mouth twisted. His blue eyes blazed.

She knew she was flirting with danger. He was giving fair warning. Anger was coming off his lean powerful body in waves. "I'm sorry, Josh. I don't want to have words with you. I must go." She made to turn away to go back into the house, only to her stupendous shock he spun her around, pulling her to him in one supremely smooth, controlling gesture.

"Josh!" Totally thrown off her guard, Clio felt a

great coursing of blood through her body. Every sense reeled.

His mouth so swiftly and completely took hers it burned up every ounce of resistance. She was flooded with excitement, robbed of all breath, all strength, willpower. Her mouth had a life of its own. It was responding to such a voluptuous invasion as if she had no other choice. Her surrender was total. Truth was, he had captured her to the core of her being.

She was gasping when he released her, losing an astonishing sense of the security and *rightness* she had felt with her body pressed against his. Was it possible she had chosen Joshua Hart above all others all those years ago?

"Maybe that will take care of Keeley for you and the rest of your guests," he bit out, furious with himself for losing it. Only Clio Templeton could have robbed him of his armour. Only Clio had the woman magic to lead him on. That humbling piece of knowledge stuck in his throat. He didn't *want* a woman to possess him, to turn him into some sort of a slave. He *hated* losing the cool order he had imposed on himself and his life.

As physically strong as he was, his heart was fluttering in his chest and there was a roaring in his ears. He stood there, aware they had created a rivetting spectacle. It would have taken everyone by surprise, indeed shock. Some of the guests were standing stunned yet Clio, with her beautiful head held high, walked back very calmly into the grand living room and didn't look back.

CHAPTER TWO

IT WAS close on a fortnight later before Josh called in on his mentor. Gossip in the town had been rife after the incident with Clio at the gala function. People talked endlessly and breathlessly at dinner parties, in the streets, over back fences. One kiss, it seemed, had created a sensation. All allowances had been made for Clio. He was the one who had overstepped the mark. Big time. Certainly he had acted under compulsion and paid for it. He couldn't get that kiss out of his mind. The best strategy seemed to him to stay away from the house.

Meg Palmer, the housekeeper, greeted him at the door. "Josh!" She embraced him briefly, then let him go. Never pushed it. It saddened her greatly to know Josh Hart as a boy had had little contact with warmth and affection and the gentling effect of a woman's touch. Meg was a short, sturdy woman of robust good health, with twinkling hazel eyes and a shock of soft iron-grey curls.

"How's business?" She looked him up and down with pleasure. She well remembered how desperately unhappy and out of control Josh had been as a boy. But hadn't he *grown*! These days he was a man of achievements. Meg felt as proud of Josh as his mentor, Leo, did.

"I do the best I can, Meg." Josh bestowed on her one of his beautiful white smiles. He rarely smiled, which was a pity, but he had a dry sense of humour. "How's Leo today?" No rhetorical question. He was waiting on the answer.

"Really looking forward to your visit," she assured him. "He's in the study, waiting. Feel like a cup of coffee?"

"You've baked your chocolate brownies?"

"I have indeed." She caught him by the arm. "You and Miss Clio made up yet?"

He responded with wry humour, not the cold anger most people would have elicited. "Meg you know damned well Clio and I aren't at any place where we make up."

"I know nothing of the kind." Meg searched his eyes. "You're as good as anyone. Better!"

"Ah, Meg," he groaned. "Not everyone is like you."

"Too true!" Meg laughed to lighten things up. "Trust me, Josh," she added very gently as he moved off to the study. Meg had heard all the gossip about that sizzling kiss but she had the good sense not to mention it.

Josh gave her a backward wave, but didn't answer. At sixty, Meg still believed in fairy-tales.

Approaching his seventh-fifth year, up until fairly recent times Leo Templeton could easily have passed for a man ten years younger. Now there were visible signs of ageing, worsening osteoporosis and general ill health. It hurt Josh to bear witness to Leo's decline. Leo may have slowed down physically, but nothing was going to slow his brain. Leo turned from looking out through the open French doors that led onto the rose garden to greet his protégée.

"Josh, my boy!"

"Please don't get up." Josh moved towards the regal silver-haired man. He put his hands on the back of Leo's big swivel armchair, pushing it back in front of his desk. Obviously Leo hadn't experienced the full heat of the gossip or he had elected to ignore it as a bizarre aberration. His manner was the same as ever.

Leo's study was a huge room, dominated by walls of floor-to-ceiling bookcases containing a vast assortment of literature—law books galore, biographies, histories, great fiction, popular fiction, the best in crime, courtroom dramas, thrillers. You name it, Leo had it in his bookcases. He knew because he had borrowed very many a book. There was a burgundy leather sofa and a pair of matching leather armchairs; a good-sized coffee table where Meg could set out tea, coffee and accompaniments.

"Thank you, Josh. I'm so pleased to see you. I've been missing our conversations. There was some talk you were out of town?" In truth Leo felt near starved of the stimulation he felt in his protégée's company. Of course he knew better than anyone of the bond between Clio and Josh but he had long since acted on it. Much as he admired Josh, his chances of ever getting close to his beautiful granddaughter were very slim indeed. Regretfully, he couldn't countenance Josh Hart as a suitor for all his brilliance. He knew nothing of Josh's bloodline—the single mother's drug overdose was bad, father unknown, no history—so he had to be rejected.

"Just scouting around," Josh said, taking his usual armchair facing his mentor.

"So what's in the briefcase?" Leo's lined face was alight with interest. Josh and his endeavours were keeping him alive.

Josh began to unzip the large black case. "I have some plans here for Aquarius." He named the beautiful tropical island Leo had bought many years before. "We did talk briefly about it some months back, remember?'

Leo nodded. "I had a notion this was coming." Josh was always brimming with ideas, projects, plans. He was immensely talented and energetic. Just like he himself had once been. Every last one of the young man's projects for which he, as Josh's mentor, had laid out a lot of capital had paid off big time. So young to be so successful! So young to make a sizeable fortune! Josh reminded him of himself. He had long since faced the fact his son, Lyle, who stood to inherit, so much didn't have a head for business. Sometimes it didn't work out so well for heirs when their forebears were the ones who had made all the money.

While Leo ruminated, Josh was busy pulling out maps, blueprints, architectural drawings, floor plans. He set them on the desk. "I think it's time for a resort complex on the island, Leo. A resort where guests can swim, sail, scuba dive, snorkel in protected waters. I have an architectural sketch here for a marina and yacht club I'd like to show you. People could sail over from the mainland and drop anchor. The other side of the island would house solar water-purification facilities among other things. We could build a splendid villa for the use of the family plus other luxury villas hidden away in the grounds for well-heeled overseas tourists."

"Not a bit ambitious?" Leo questioned, chewing at his bottom lip.

"I don't think so, Leo. Hear me out. I've done all the figures, checked out government requirements. But I do need *your* interest and approval. It's *your* island after all. But, as we agreed, it's just sitting there. If you don't think it advisable at this time, the project will go on hold. Until you *do*!" Josh suddenly laughed.

Such an attractive sound, Leo thought. Josh had taken a long time to let down his guard. But eventually it had happened. Their minds met. At least their business minds. "Then come round and spread it all out before me." Leo began to clear papers from his massive mahogany desk, shoving them into a drawer.

"You won't regret this, Leo." Josh was already on his feet, a number of wound-up rolls in his hands.

Driving towards the family home, Lyle Templeton thought it had been years since he'd had a *real* conversation with his father. He intended to have that conversation tonight. Not that there had been any estrangement as such, but things had been very different after his beloved Allegra's tragic death. Allegra had been the glue that had held father and son together. Leo had made no effort to hide the fact he disliked and distrusted Keeley right from the beginning. He had been very much against the marriage, openly questioning whether his son was, in fact, the father of Keeley's mystery baby. Now no one would ever know. Keeley had lost the child. Either she was one of the world's finest actresses or she had suffered genuine grief. As had he. So he had not only lost a second child, he had lost his beloved Clio. Clio had simply not wanted to stay in the house with Keeley. She had gone to live with Leo, who had welcomed her with wide-open arms. It was as though Allegra had returned.

Of late his father's health had been on the decline. They all saw that. The threat to family had come not from Keeley, who didn't rate, but from the youngster, Josh Hart. Leo had sponsored the boy's education, private school through university, doling out huge sums of money to partner the young entrepreneur Hart eventually became. Not that Hart wasn't brilliant—he hadn't put a foot wrong—but Lyle truly felt he had been relegated to third place in his father's life. Josh Hart had his father's ear, and mind, worse, his heart. Not *him*. His father didn't need him any more. He had Josh Hart. And another terrible worry had taken hold. For years hostile to the young man, hostility had increased to a pervading fear.

Hart had ambitions to take his beautiful daughter.

Hart was dangerous. He always had been. Bad blood.

Hart's Porsche was parked in the drive. He'd been reliably told Hart was looking at some property further north. Lyle would have found out he was back had he rung ahead to say he was coming, but he had wanted his visit to be in the nature of a pleasant surprise. Hart had beaten him to it. Thank God Clio wasn't at home. One night a month she had dinner with Lisa and the family. Lisa was another one blind to any character flaws in Josh Hart. She thought the world of him. Hart had saved baby Ella's life.

* * *

To his surprise Lyle found the front door open. He called, "Hello," but received no reply. He stood for a few minutes, frowning. He fully expected Mrs Palmer to rush to the entrance, an apology on her lips. She really should have been on hand. He moved further down the hall, becoming aware of raised voices. They were coming from his father's study. Both voices were recognisable. Something was the matter. He was abruptly furious. Joshua Hart was in the house. The very idea put him on extreme edge.

When he arrived outside the open study door, he was shocked to see his father lying flat on the floor, his striped blue and white cotton shirt open. Hart was on his knees, leaning over him, pressing down on Leo's chest with both hands. Mrs Palmer was standing nearby, her face ashen, her hands clasped as if in prayer.

"What the devil is going on here?" Anger engulfed him. He was shouting, he was so perturbed. Losing Allegra had almost sent him stark raving mad, now his father?

No one answered him. He may not have been there. "Is Dad having a heart attack?"

Belatedly Mrs Palmer found her voice. "I'm so sorry, Mr Lyle. I've called the emergency number. Paramedics are on the way."

"So what the hell is Hart doing? Shouldn't he be leaving my father well alone until they arrive?"

"Mr Leo was unconscious," Meg Palmer explained, feeling acute pity for Lyle. "He wasn't breathing. Josh has the training. CPR is a life-saving technique. Think about it, now, Mr Lyle." Lyle Templeton looked like he wanted to order Josh out of the house.

"I'm thinking about what *caused* it," Lyle choked. "Did Dad and Hart get into some kind of an argument? What are all those rolls on Dad's desk? They look like architectural drawings to me. One of Hart's schemes, trying to involve my father."

"That's the ambulance now, Meg." Hart looked up from exhaling breath into Leo's slack mouth. He ignored Lyle entirely.

"I'll let them in."

"The damned door is *open*," Lyle exploded. "I need some explanations here."

He wasn't about to get one from Josh Hart.

* * *

Clio took the call on her mobile, even though they had started dinner. It had to be an emergency. It was her father, telling her to return home immediately. "It's your grandfather," he said, breaking into a harsh sob. Then he hung up without another word.

She made it home in record time, risking being caught for speeding. Leo had been taken ill. That much was certain. She arrived at the mansion just as the ambulance, presumably with Leo on board, turned out onto the road. For one mad moment she considered flagging them down and then thought better of it. Gravel spewed from the tyres as she pulled right to the base of the short fight of steps that led to the house.

Her father met her at the door, anger in his voice such as she had never heard before. "Hart is here."

"Yes, I saw his Porsche." She wasn't aware Josh was back in town. Josh moved around a lot, scouting out land for future development. There was the possibility too he had wanted to stay clear of all the gossip that had engulfed them.

Who could blame him? "Tell me quickly. What's happened? I almost ran into the ambulance."

"They're taking Dad to the hospital for *expert* attention. Not Hart's. He's not saying much other than Dad had a heart attack, but my suspicion is he and Dad were having a furious argument. From what I can make out, Hart wants to take over Aquarius. Build some sort of a tourist complex. Dad has never wanted that."

That was certainly true. Leo had owned the island for many years but had never done anything with it. "I suggest you take it easy, Dad," Clio said, knowing her father was not the man he had once been. "This is all supposition. Where is Josh? And Meg? Meg will know. We need to get to the hospital."

Her father gave an enraged snort. "You know as well as I do, Clio, that Mrs Palmer dotes on that dangerous young man. She'd say anything to cover for him."

"Please, Dad." Clio's face twisted in pain and grief. "Let's establish the facts before you go off on Josh." She broke away from her father's trembling arms, hurrying towards her grandfather's study.

She found Josh and Meg sitting in total silence at the outdoor setting a few feet from Leo's study. Both stood up as she all but flew through the French doors, followed by her father. Meg went to her, tears glittering in her eyes. Josh stood back, as inscrutable as ever.

Always the quickening pulse, the electric buzz in her presence. Even at this gut-wrenching time with worry about Leo.

There was a gentleness to Clio's voice as she took Meg into a comforting hug. "What happened?" At the same time she looked over Meg's cloud of fluffy curls to Josh. He stood tall and aloof.

"Mr Leo and Josh were having a conference," Meg said in a shaky voice. "I'd served them coffee. Some time later I heard Josh yell to me to call for an ambulance. Mr Leo had collapsed. I wasted no time, Clio," she assured Clio defensively. "The ambulance arrived a short time after your father. A paramedic took over from Josh, who'd been giving your grandfather CPR. Mr

Leo appeared to regain consciousness, and they rushed him off."

"That's *your* account of it, is it?" Lyle turned almost violently on the trembling Meg. It was obvious he was getting into *serious* stride. "That young man over there has a criminal record."

"Oh, Dad, *shut it*!" Clio said. "Josh does *not* have a criminal record."

"Well, it's a far from commendable one," Lyle said, his feelings running out of control.

Josh moved, six feet three of leashed power. "I'll go," he said, addressing Clio for the first time. "You don't want me here."

"You're so right about that!" Lyle was back to shouting, eyeing the young man with great disdain. "I'd be very happy not to see you again. And don't go taking your papers with you. I need to go into this matter more fully."

"Well, you *do* have a history of mistrusting me." Josh moved into the study in such a way the older man fell back. Hart's height and physical grace only served to make him seem even more dangerous. "The bad kid is the bad man?" Josh queried ironically. "Or is it the old adage that a savage is a savage is a savage right?"

"Absolutely." Lyle watched impotently as Josh collected his papers and shoved them into a big black briefcase.

"I'm sorry, Clio," Josh said, preparing to leave. He could see her acute distress. Her golden skin had a distinct pallor and her eyes glittered with unshed tears. Nothing he could do about it. His feelings for her, his fantasy life with her, especially since that kiss, were now completely out of hand. He should *never* have kissed her. That had been sheer madness. Her father's hostility towards him, always in evidence, had escalated to hatred. "Leo's bad turn came right out of the blue."

"So *you* say!" Lyle broke in furiously. His memory too was seared by *that* kiss his beautiful daughter and Hart had shared. To his stunned eyes it had looked devastatingly passionate.

"Please, Dad." Clio held up a hand. "You're not even giving Josh a chance to speak."

"Trouble comes naturally to Josh Hart." Lyle

was shocked by his own attack but unable to contain it.

"I'll come to the car with you, Josh." Clio turned back to speak to Meg. "Sit down before you fall down, Meg. I'll make some tea when I come back. Then we should go to the hospital."

Meg drew a deep, steadying breath. "I'll make the tea, love. You go with Josh."

"Listen, Clio…" Her father tried to detain her.

"*You* listen, Dad. I'm not a child. I'm twenty-four years of age. I pick my own friends. You can't run my life."

"No need to speak to me like that, Clio," Lyle protested, deeply hurt and doubly enraged his daughter should take Hart's side. It was unforgivable.

"I'll be back, Dad," she promised by way of consolation.

They were out in the warm night with the golden moon of the tropics hanging low. They walked towards Josh's Porsche. Or rather Josh was striding purposefully while she was at a near run to keep up. "Go back inside, Clio," he said, his voice a taut order.

"Didn't you hear me? I pick my own friends," she told him with a spurt of anger.

Josh used the remote button to unlock his car. "Only we're *not* friends, Clio, are we?" His fine white teeth gritted. "Leo set the rules long ago. I'm supposed to respect you, Clio. Keep my distance. It was made very plain to me without any need for words you were off limits to the likes of me. I was not to make the slightest attempt to get close to the Templeton heiress or I would be cut adrift. Leo has his ruthless streak."

"Well, then, you made a monumental mistake kissing me, didn't you?" There was a world of frustrated challenge in her voice. How many dozen times a day had she relived those wildly tempestuous moments? "God knows, it's been the talk of the town even if my grandfather elected not to talk to me about it."

Josh responded, "Leo has his reasons for everything. He chose to ignore the gossip as the best strategy. He didn't mention anything to me either. That would make too much of it. The incident has been brushed under the carpet where it belongs, not brought out into the open. That's Leo's way."

"Okay, so I recognize it."

"So can you recognize also that I've had a hard time with my loss of control?" How could he say that when his feelings for her ran at full throttle?

"God knows, it's rare enough!" she commented with some sharpness. "What happened tonight, Josh?" she asked, her voice strained. "Was there an argument? Did Leo become upset? Those plans in there, were they for a development on Aquarius?"

"They are," he clipped off in a deadly quiet tone.

"And Leo *wanted* to see them and hear your proposal?" she asked, perplexed. "Leo has long been against tourist development. We all know that. It's just as Dad said."

The full moon revealed the tension on his strongly sculpted face. "Maybe, unlike *you*, Clio," he said cuttingly, "Leo believed in me.

He believed I could bring the right sort of project off. Now we know *your* thoughts and your father's on the subject, you really should go back inside."

He was staring down at her in his imperious fashion. "Excuse me, I live here," she reminded him, as on edge as he was.

"Of course you do," he agreed tonelessly. "All the more reason for you to go inside. I'm in no doubt that if Leo dies I'll be an exile from this house. Not that I've ever been a welcome guest. I couldn't possibly make *that* transition. I know how much you and your father love Leo. I feel deeply sorry for you both, but I should prepare you for possible bad news. Leo may not survive. If his brain has sustained damage, he wouldn't want to survive. He was unconscious. Not breathing. I administered CPR and kept at it until the medics arrived. End of story. And another piece of advice—it might be best for you if you stay away from me, Clio. Contact only brings grief. Go back into the house now. I'm sure you want to get to the hospital."

She went. She dared not stay a moment longer

before she beat out her sense of utter helpless-
ness and frustration against the steely wall of
his chest.

The richest man in town had died; so rich even
the rich called him rich. Accordingly almost
the entire township turned out to lay Leo
Templeton to rest. It poured with rain yet most
people elected to attend the graveside service
when Clio wouldn't have blamed anyone for not
wanting to stand in the heavy rain. As it happened, just about everyone did, except for those
well on in years. People were not only determined
to pay their last respects, they had to be seen to
be doing it. Leo had died in the ambulance on
his way to hospital from his massive heart attack.
   Most people would take their leave, but family
and close friends had been invited back to the
house. The same sad old ritual. The gathering.
The eating, drinking, even the subdued laughter.
It didn't seem appropriate to Clio. She hadn't
cried through the service. Bizarrely she had
to fight back a laugh because the mourners in
their black clothes with raised black umbrellas

put her in mind of colonies of tropical fruit bats. Part hysteria, she knew. Anyway, she did her crying in private. Stoic in adversity. It could have been the Templeton mantra. Not that there had been much in the way of financial adversity. But clearly money wasn't everything. The rich couldn't escape the dying of the light any more than the poor, though the funerals of the rich usually drew much bigger crowds.

Directly opposite, the Crowley family had turned out in force. Old Paddy Crowley was suited up like Darth Vader. Vince and Jimmy were making a ridiculous show of sadness. Real tears welled up in poor Susan's eyes. When she could, she was going to have to do something about Susan Crowley's situation. Women's affairs, the family courts, had always interested her. She had spent enough time in the backwaters of Templetons. She had to take the plunge into real life. Even deeply distressed, she couldn't help the flare-up of irritation at the way Jimmy kept staring at her. Funny how she despised Jimmy yet she liked and felt sorry for him at the same time. The Crowleys had to be mad to cling to the idea she and Jimmy would make a match of it. That was well and truly burying one's head in the sand.

It was impossible to miss Josh, even though he stood well back in the crowd. He hadn't bothered with an umbrella. He wore an expensive black raincoat over his clothes. The rain had drenched his blond hair, darkening the colour.

"What's *he* doing here?" Lyle demanded angrily of his daughter, as everyone began to head for their cars. The tension in him was so palpable it hung around them like a cloud. "I tell you I won't have it," he declared, hostile even in deep distress. "He killed Dad. You know it. I know it. The town knows it."

Clio bit her lip until a speck of blood appeared. "Only because *you* let the rumour get started, Dad," she said, feeling tremendous shame. "I never would have believed my own dear father could be so vindictive. Josh Hart has never hurt you. He saved Ella's life. We simply don't *know* what happened. I think it highly unlikely Josh would have persisted in trying to sell any project

to Leo he was against. That wouldn't have happened. We both knew Leo. Usually he and Josh
were of one mind. If anyone could have swung
it with Grandad, it would have been Josh. I think
I might ask you why Keeley didn't come. She
didn't want to get wet?"

Lyle's expression was mortified. "Keeley
wanted to be here but she's taken Dad's death
unexpectedly hard. I was the one who told her
she needn't come to the graveside service, but
she *will* come to the house."

"A stellar effort! You don't know how much
joy that gives me, Dad. There was no love lost
between Leo and Keeley." She knew she should
have let it slide, but she was so overwrought she
didn't. She had adored her grandfather, even
though she had lived with his benign domination. She hadn't been with him when he'd died.
That was a deep grief.

"Why are you saying this now, Clio?" Lyle
asked in anguish.

"Sorry, Dad. We're both terribly upset. People
tend to say what they *really* mean when they're
horrendously upset. Go back to the car. The worst

of the rain appears to be over. There's a chink of blue over there. The sun is breaking through. I want to have a quick word with Josh."

Lyle lifted his head to the heavens. "Lord, give me strength!" he implored. "I love you, Clio. You're my only child. I'm only trying to protect you."

Clio gently touched his arm. "Try protecting yourself, Dad," she advised, and turned away.

She had to run across the grass, her high heels sinking into the wet turf and hindering her progress. "Josh!" she called out. "Please wait."

He made her come to him. When she was within a couple of feet of him he moved to take her arm and draw her beneath the shelter of a massive Moreton Bay fig. One of the biggest and most robust trees in the world, its giant roots sprawled over a wide area, its great prop roots supporting the trunk. Josh chose a clear section for them to stand.

"Thank you for coming," she said breathlessly. Her heart was thrumming. There was a dryness in her throat. He meant so much to her yet he looked so unapproachable, commanding, austere.

His blue eyes transfixed her where she stood. She had never ever seen such an intensely focused regard.

"Why would I not?" Josh answered. "Not even your father putting it around town I caused Leo's death would have prevented me coming. I'm glad Bart McMannus didn't share his views. A warning you might pass on to your father. He had better keep out of my way. This isn't a good time for me either."

The wind blew a little flurry of spent yellow leaves onto his wide shoulders. He left them there. "I'm so sorry, Josh." Her voice cracked with emotion. "Losing my mother all but finished Dad off."

"Keeley will do the rest," he stated bluntly.

Clio gave a deep sigh. "It's always a shock when people reveal aspects of themselves that were never previously there. Dad's mind has become a little skewed. You have to understand the way Leo thinking the world of you impacted on my father. You weren't family, but Leo loved you."

"Nonsense, Clio," he responded bluntly. "The only person who has ever loved me was my mother. Leo and I shared similar aims and interests. I respected his business acumen greatly. I acknowledge I have a great deal to thank him for. But you could never say he loved me. That's vastly overstating it."

"No, it's not." She swayed a little shakily. Straight away he reached for her, steadying her with his hands on her shoulders. There was great intimacy in the gesture. The air around them turned as electric, as if they were caught in the middle of a severe thunderstorm. "You don't *want* to be loved, Josh." Her gaze was at once compassionate and challenging. "You have plenty of women in the town *in love* with you."

"And not one I want." He abruptly released her, thinking of the flame inside him that would never burn out.

Clio found herself pleading. "Don't shut me out, Josh." She felt so sad and lonely it was all she could do not to break down and weep.

If only he would hold me. He was immensely strong.

"Clio, for God's sake!" For the first time he showed real emotion, as though he had flashed onto her feelings. "I'm trying to discourage you from making a big mistake."

"Ah, to hell with that!" The words flew from her lips. "What mistake would that *be*, Josh?"

His sculpted mouth took on a bitter curl. "You know. Better to stick to the *noli me tangere* policy." It hurt him terribly to see her beautiful face grow even paler, but he couldn't possibly expose her to more trauma. She must have found all the gossip about them acutely embarrassing, yet she seemed to think it was okay they become close. Many people in the town thought just the opposite. Not that he gave a damn about them. His only concern was to protect Clio from all harm and spurious gossip. He knew she had an enemy in her stepmother. Keeley wouldn't think twice about hurting Clio, adding embellishments to all the malicious whispers. The way to protect Clio was for him to conceal his true feelings. Not all that difficult, surely? He had done just that for almost his entire life.

Right versus wrong; love versus hate. He wasn't sure what it was he felt for Clio. He had precious little experience of what people called love. He only knew he wanted her more than he wanted anything in the world. Was *that* love? Was love a driving *need*? Was love immense pleasure in the sight and sound of her? He would do anything to keep her safe. He would punish anyone who hurt her. Was *that* love? What did he know about love anyway? He knew a great deal about pain and the multiple ways it was inflicted. He knew about suffering and being stoic. He knew about lust, the lust that had been felt for him as a handsome boy. He knew about learning to protect himself. He'd become better than good at that. He knew about losing his only parent before he could possibly look after himself. Love simply hadn't existed right through the years that had formed him. Maybe he wasn't allowed to love? Maybe happiness would forever elude him? What he did know was that love came with loss.

Clio looked up at him as he stood there in brooding silence. "What are you thinking about, Josh?" she asked quietly. "What is it you're looking for?" She continued to stare up at him as though determined to get the truth out of him.

His brow knitted. "I'm looking not to cause

you further harm, Clio. If you turn your head, you'll see quite a few people are staring our way. Your father is standing beside his car, talking to the Crowleys, who really are scumbags. But it seems they're more acceptable than I am. Old Paddy with his death's-head grin. How do you stand nice Jimmy never taking his eyes off you? The way I see it, your father is anxious for you to return to the fold. Is he so blind he can't see what the Crowleys are all about? I might have to exclude Jimmy. He has no real sense of himself. He just does what he's told."

"Dad likes to see the best in people," Clio offered, halfheartedly.

"It's an easy option." Josh's response was cynical. "He condones the likes of the Crowleys, yet he truly believes I'm no good."

Clio's brilliant dark eyes flashed. "I think it more likely he believes you *too* good," she said spiritedly. "It's struck me recently that much as I loved Leo and I love my father, both men in my life have demanded total allegiance from me."

His beautiful mouth twisted. "So you've finally figured it out?"

"Do you feel contempt for me?"

"God, no!" he said explosively. He was mad with wanting her.

"I'm glad of that. But I never rebelled, did I? Leo ruled us with an iron fist wrapped in a velvet glove. He had control of you through his trusteeship. You were just a boy and you were required to tread a straight line. You must have had a lot of strength even then to maintain it after you'd virtually run wild. As for me, I'm not finding excuses, but I lost my mother at a critical time. A girl needs her mother. I know you're very brave, Josh. I know you've had to gird yourself in armour to survive. I know we've got a bond. *I* want it to go deeper. I know *exactly* what I want. I want us to be friends. Don't let everyone else win, Josh. I'm not nine. I'm a woman now. I intend taking my life into my own two hands."

"Then you'd better be prepared for a battle," he said. He looked down into her beautiful face. Her flawless skin was much paler than usual but glowing and dewy in the rain. Little tendrils of her dark hair curled around her temples and wisped out onto her cheeks. "We can't make this right, Clio. Things have to settle. A lot of people feed on gossip. They've had a field day in recent times. I'm so sorry for that. Now they've been given the idea I was in some way responsible for Leo's death."

Hot tears sprang into her eyes. "Then they're very bad judges of character."

"Maybe." He gazed over her head. "Your dad has grown tired of waiting, it seems. He's coming towards us. Don't let him get here, Clio," he advised. "I'd like to see him hit the turf. But I'd hate you to see it."

There was a coiled tension in his superbly fit body. She could see it was straining for release. No way was she going to get Josh into trouble. And it could happen. "It's okay, Josh," she said swiftly. "I'll go." She turned back for a moment, her beautiful eyes so full of sorrow he was desperate to offer whatever comfort he could, but knew he couldn't. Certainly not here. "I had hoped you'd come back to the house," she said, "but that's out of the question?"

"Absolutely." The dark timbre of his voice was as dry as ash.

She moved on. She had so wanted to give Josh *her* stamp of approval. She knew Leo had left the family home to her. She was expected to fill it with her children, Templeton descendants. "I'll give it a little time," she called back, lifting a hand in farewell.

CHAPTER THREE

LEO TEMPLETON had appointed one of his closest friends, Supreme Court Judge Henry Morgenstern, as executor of his will. The family had to wait a day for the judge to arrive, and now various members of the high-finance Templeton clan that counted in the children, grandchildren, cousins, even second cousins, were gathered in Leo's study, with Henry seated behind the massive partner's desk, with its elaborately carved lion's paws for feet. Henry had pushed some papers to one side, before polishing away an invisible speck on his glasses. Next, he looked up over the top of his spectacles at those present, all of whom he knew. "Not much here you don't know, my dear friends." At least *one* surprise, however.

Inside Clio was quaking. She was certain Leo would have made mention of Josh in his will.

Now she awaited confirmation with very real trepidation. Her father had it in for Josh, and no mistake. She knew the root cause was jealousy. And a lot of it was Leo's fault. Leo had treated Josh in a different way from her father. Her father might lack Leo's brilliance and Midas touch—he didn't really understand money, probably because he'd never had to make it—but he had always applied himself very diligently to everything that was asked of him. With Josh Hart increasingly on the scene, her father might well have perceived himself not as Leo's *only* son but a second string.

Such things happened. There was nothing ordinary about Josh. He was as exotic as a young lion. That had appealed greatly to her grandfather, who in his youth had exuded great physical attraction along with immense vigour and vitality. These days, with his marriage moving inexorably towards divorce, her father would believe his life was getting emptier and emptier with every passing day. Once a divorce was in full swing, he could go traveling—open his heart, his mind and his eyes. He could find the *right* woman. It wasn't out of the question. He was much too young to shut down. There had to be light at the end of the tunnel. One had to believe it. Clio made up her mind she would have a long talk with her father.

He was speaking now, his tone bombastic. "I'd appreciate it, Henry, if you'd read my father's will to us *now*."

Clio caught her breath. The relatives looked shocked. Lyle was always a gentleman, sweet, with exceedingly good manners.

"No point in delaying." Lyle sat virtually centre stage with Keeley on one side, overdressed for a will-reading, an extremely valuable necklet of South Sea pearls around her throat, which she kept fingering to make sure it was still there, and his beautiful daughter in a simple dark grey silk dress on the other. Leo's two sisters, married rich, handsome women, perfectly attired, sat in the second row. Both lived in Melbourne, Sarah with her retired neurosurgeon husband, Delphine with her husband, a retired investment banker. Other members of the extended family, a small crowd, had pulled up chairs, positioning themselves where best they could.

"Of course, Lyle." Judge Morgenstern tolerated the terseness of "young" Lyle's request, because he could see how tremendously upset Leo's only son was. He knew well in advance this wasn't going to be easy. In fact, he anticipated a big problem. Someone definitely wouldn't like this. Maybe the lot of them.

"If you would, please, Henry." Clio gave him her lovely smile, making up for her father's curt tone. She was clearly embarrassed. The judge smiled back. He was very fond of Clio. She needed to get away from her father's influence. For that matter, the judge considered Leo had done his best to clip Clio's wings. Clio was a very clever young woman. She had done extremely well at university, only it had become glaringly apparent Leo couldn't bear to have his granddaughter out of his sight. In the Templeton family, going back many long years, *sons* were the thing. Daughters had different roles entirely.

By the time Henry had finished the reading, a kind of chaos reigned. Lyle was clenching the armrests of his chair so tightly his knuckles showed white, while rage had put red into his handsome face. His whole life had gone to pot! And he knew how it had happened.

It was painfully obvious to all that Lyle was trying desperately to keep himself together. No comfort from his wife, who was smiling and staring upward with an expression of near ecstasy, as though seeing a splendid vision. Not the religious kind.

"Do you mean to tell me Leo left that young man *Aquarius*?" Delphine asked her great-niece in wonderment. They all knew Josh's history and how Leo had taken the "bad boy in town" under his mantle.

"Don't forget the rest of it!" Lyle shouted, shoving his armchair back so violently Clio had to move fast to prevent it ramming Great-Aunt Delphine's distinguished husband, who was looking aghast at Lyle's lack of decorum and control. The Lyle they had always known had morphed into someone else entirely.

"Not that I don't accept it!" said Great-Aunt Delphine, patting her husband's knee consolingly.

It *had* taken a hard knock. "Leo always did know what he was doing. I believe the young man has turned out quite brilliantly!"

"For God's sake!" Disillusionment and anger burst from Lyle's throat. "Give me the will, Henry. I want to read this for myself."

The judge sat straighter. "I assure you everything is in perfect order, Lyle." His tone made it perfectly plain he wasn't going to accept any more rudeness. Nevertheless, he passed the document over to Lyle, who took in most of it, in seconds, then promptly pitched it on the floor. "This is proof positive Dad was losing his mind. Or Hart had so manipulated him, perhaps intimidated him, so as he left him the island?"

Henry Morgenstern employed his judicial voice, which usually compelled instant attention, certainly in the courtroom though strangely enough not in his home, where his wife ruled. "*No one* intimidated Leo, as you very well know. Leo had enormous faith in young Hart to make a success of himself. He considered Hart had a great future."

"But this is a young man who came from the wrong side of the tracks," Lyle appealed to everyone in near despair.

"People still concerned about bloodlines, are they?" Keeley piped up, having none to speak of.

It didn't seem as if Lyle had registered the fact he was the major beneficiary, which made him an extremely rich man. Lyle's entire focus was on Josh Hart's legacy, which didn't strike anyone else as being over the top but was still worth a handsome sum. Clio had been left the Templeton historic home and a cool $100 million as well as an apartment in Sydney and the beach house on Queensland's Gold Coast. Leo's sisters were handsomely rewarded, with personal effects for the husbands. The younger members of the extended family didn't go short either. Henry came in for Leo's splendid collection of bronze sculptures. Meg Palmer could shut up shop tomorrow. Various charities were generously endowed. Substantial grants to the Queensland University in Brisbane, the James Cook University of North Queensland. All would be thrilled.

Only one very vocal exception. Lyle Templeton

was looking and acting as though he had been left without a dime and nowhere to turn but the streets.

"I'll fight this," he vowed.

"How smart is that?" questioned Keeley, one painted eyebrow shooting up.

"My dear fellow, you *won't* win." Henry was as surprised as anyone other than Clio by Lyle's violent and irrational reaction.

Clio took her father's arm, persuading him to sit down again. Josh's legacy of Aquarius blew her father's crazy accusations out of the water. Yet she was filled with pity, knowing her father would have trouble getting over this.

"Gracious, Lyle, anyone would think you'd been treated badly," Keeley said in her breathy voice. "I suppose it's all taxed?"

No one answered. No one had taken to Lyle's second wife, a gold-digger if ever there was one. With a wife like that, it was more than possible Lyle was suffering a delayed mid-life crisis.

Lyle had stormed off, paying no attention whatever to Keeley, who followed much more slowly, determined to have a word with her stepdaughter. Clio was so beautiful even when grief-stricken that it made Keeley really cross.

"Poor Lyle isn't at all fond of Josh, is he?" she offered dryly.

"No, he isn't," Clio admitted. "Whatever you do, Keeley, I'd advise you to keep your distance."

"Excuse me?" Keeley gave an excellent impression of a deeply offended woman.

"I don't want to see my father made a fool of. Keep your distance from Josh Hart."

Keeley threw back her head, giving a near braying laugh. "Phone calls okay?" she asked breezily.

Clio felt a stab of revulsion. "Would you care to explain that?"

"Do I really need to? Josh rings me. I ring him. Nothing wrong with that, my dear. It is the twenty-first century. We're just friends."

Anger overtook Clio. "You might want to be friends, but it's not going to happen. You're a married woman. Your husband is my father. I'm only masquerading as a nice person, Keeley.

Shame my father and you'd better look out."
Clio's dark eyes flashed.

The conviction in Clio's voice got Keeley's attention. "Good Lord, I'm beginning to see you in a different light, my dear. Of course it's not every day a girl gets $100 million. But I'm no fool. You might do a great job of hiding it, but you're mad about Josh yourself. Now you have so much money, Josh might very well *fake* an interest in you. Gorgeous Josh is a bit of a sociopath, don't you think? He can't *care* for anyone. His heart is like hammered steel. He doesn't mind sex, though," she gurgled. "I know for a fact he fancies me."

Clio endeavoured to put a dent in her stepmother's supreme self-confidence. "Sorry, Keeley. You're too old."

Keeley's red mouth fell open, but very oddly she didn't argue. "And *you*, girlie, aren't up to speed." She clapped a hard hand on her stepdaughter's arm, leaving the marks of her fingers, before heading out the door.

At least she'd had the last word. That was something. She would call Josh as soon as she got home. Congratulate him on becoming overnight a fine, upright citizen. He would take the princely legacy Leo Templeton had left him and build on it. Josh Hart was going places. Wouldn't it be brilliant to go with him? That parting shot from her stepdaughter had hit home. Obviously she needed a touch-up with Botox. It had to be the great scientific breakthrough of the twentieth century.

Within an hour the family had dispersed, except for Clio's great-aunts and their husbands, who were staying over until the morrow when Tom would drive them to the airport to begin their trip back home to Melbourne. Before he left in the chauffeured Rolls, Henry had a word with Clio. "I thought Leo had quite a few more years left in him."

"It's a shock to us all, Henry. You must have noticed Dad really has it in for Josh Hart?"

Henry pulled a wry face. "Most unfortunate, and, it must be said, unreasonable. All information to hand confirms Hart has graduated to dazzling success as an entrepreneur. A 'young man of integrity' is the word. One wonders how he's going to react to his good fortune." Henry focused his shrewd, kindly eyes on Clio's face. She was Allegra all over again. The same haunting beauty, the same look of class. Henry thought Clio would make a good fist of building on her inherited fortune. Even better, her mindset was far more philanthropic than Leo's. It would be very interesting to see what Clio Templeton would do next.

The family retired not all that long after dinner. They had an 8 o'clock flight in the morning. Clio decided to ring Josh. She thought it best if she was the one to tell him of his inheritance before he received official confirmation. Was it likely she could be telling him something he already knew? Leo had never mentioned to her that Josh was in his will. She had never dreamt of asking. But had Josh? He had known there would be no problem starting the project on Aquarius. Had he known in advance Leo meant to leave him the island? Had he confidently expected a windfall when Leo died? She felt racked by doubts. Josh had big plans. And Josh was a man who'd had plenty of practice keeping his plans close to his chest.

In Leo's study she punched in the numbers of Josh's mobile. No problem to find it. Leo kept records of everything. She had, in fact, committed Josh's landline and mobile numbers to memory when he'd shifted into his penthouse. He'd had a top architect who worked all over South East Asia design the outstanding, modernistic complex. He and Leo had been joint partners in the very successful venture.

Her hand was shaking. Her whole body was shaking. It was just the same as when she'd been a child. Some part of her was thrilled by Josh, while another part was sensitive to the dark places in him. That would explain the tight control and the formidability of his demeanour. What had happened to him as a child she didn't want to think about. She knew absolutely *nothing* about abuse but Josh had lived with the terrible reality. All the coping mechanisms he would have had

to employ were still in place. Josh wasn't about
to reveal himself to a woman.

Josh wasn't about to reveal himself to *her*.

Keeley decided all she had to do was wait for
someone to go into or out of the classy apartment
complex where Josh lived. It took less than five
minutes. A young man and woman, arms linked,
studied her as she stood at the glass entry as if
ready to walk in.

She didn't know them. They didn't appear to
know her. Many affluent Southerners bought
holiday apartments in this glorious part of the
world. Naturally her self-assurance and the styl-
ish way she was dressed was more than sufficient
for them to return her smiling, confident "Good
evening".

So far so good. She knew she was taking an
incredible risk, coming here, but she needed to
see Josh on his own. She didn't doubt that, given
the opportunity, she could whip up enough sexual
excitement for it to go somewhere. Preferably
Josh's bed. She knew perfectly well he didn't
ignore women—he had a tremendous sexuality

about him—even if those women didn't live in town. Occasionally a name popped up. She knew his various affairs were no more than passing. The right woman could change all that. The job would require a real pro like her.

Josh's phone was engaged the first time Clio rang. She gave it fifteen minutes then called again. Still engaged, probably business. Business, business, business. She'd had a lifetime of it with her grandfather. There was nothing to stop her going over to Josh's apartment. She had never been there. She hadn't been invited. But she had pored over all the early drafts for the building, then the master plan. Obviously Josh was at home so she could buzz the penthouse. It might put him on the spot, but she didn't think he would refuse to allow her in.

She made the twenty-minute drive, parking her car across the Poinciana-lined street. There were four penthouses. Josh's was the pick of them, positioned on the far right. The lights were on. She was just opening her door to get out when in a frenzy she shut it again, recoiling into the shadows, a sob caught in her throat. For a second she closed her eyes in shock, thinking she would die of distress. In the next second, she was praying she had made a mistake.

So, anything wrong with your eyesight lately?

Josh was escorting her stepmother, dressed to kill, out of the complex. He had a guiding hand on her arm. Keeley was looking up at him, her lips moving, asking him a question? The next time they could meet? The body language from Keeley was one of intense, raw involvement. Josh kept walking her to the door, a strange look of concentration on his face. Her eyes swept over them, forced to lock in the picture they made. She had never been to Josh's apartment. But Keeley had. Lord knew how many times.

There were all kinds of sins in life, Clio thought. There was a sharp pain like a knife prick in her breast. Infidelity had to be one of the most despicable. Keeley didn't wait for life to come to her. She just kept at it and at it until she got a result. Once she had given Keeley the benefit of the doubt about her supposed pregnancy and subsequent miscarriage. Her father had thought it was the truth. Not so Leo, who had made no bones about labelling Keeley a conniving gold-digger. Now that Clio knew her stepmother so much better she realized Keeley had lied.

Striving to keep calm, she closed the fingers of her two hands around the wheel, trying to clarify her thoughts. She had two options. Confront them. Let them know precisely what she thought of them. Or drive away. Any notion of speaking to Josh faded into nothingness. The odd thing was, he didn't walk Keeley to her car, as she would have expected. She had spotted the Jaguar parked in the visitors' zone of the beautifully landscaped grounds. He remained standing outside the building, watching her move off, his blond hair shining in the exterior lights.

For the briefest of moments she clung to the belief Keeley might have been trying to compromise Josh, like she had her father, but no one could do that to Josh. He wouldn't exactly have tossed Keeley over the balcony, but he would have found a quick way to get rid of her. She had to overcome her massive upset and think coolly.

He didn't see her to her car. He's still standing there, like you, waiting for her to drive away.

Mercifully Keeley was going in the opposite direction, otherwise her headlights would have rayed into her car.

When she looked back to where Josh had been standing, he was still there, staring across the street intently. "God!" She released a strangled breath. Had he spotted her? While she remained in the car, a car had slid into the parking spot behind her. Another one was parked in front of her. The magnificent shade trees deflected most of the streetlighting.

Why don't you wave? the wicked little voice inside her head taunted.

She didn't answer. Anger was slowly devouring her. Disgust.

Go back inside, Josh.

What a fool she was, thinking Josh lived to a high standard. She had to face it squarely. Josh was a *man*. Keeley had one heck of a crush on him. All the elements were in place. Was Keeley content with living in the moment, however brief? Josh mightn't fancy Keeley, but it would be a priceless opportunity for him to get even with her father.

No, no, no! her inner voice sternly chided her. That wasn't Josh. Keeley was the predator.

God, he *had* seen her. Hands shaking, Clio turned on the ignition, put the car into drive, then pulled out of the parking spot, staring straight head. She couldn't risk a U-turn, though the street was wide enough. She had to go ahead. This was all so humiliating.

Come on, now. Settle down. Don't give in to your emotions. They're not reliable when you're in this state. What did you actually see?

Gradually she had a sense of coming more fully to herself. Josh had a place in her heart. Nothing had ever changed that. In that initial shocking instant, what she had seen seemed like a betrayal of her trust in him. Wasn't that a measure of her *feeling* for him? Distressed she had jumped to a too-obvious conclusion. She hadn't actually seen anything other than proof of Keeley's obsession. Keeley might have been desperate to make contact. Seduce Josh? She was just stupid enough to think it might work. But how had she got into the building? Josh must have allowed her in.

Think about that, girl. Don't some people in apartment buildings foolishly let down their guards?

Keeley dressed to the nines wouldn't have presented a threat to anyone going in or out. She would have waited her moment then, with a show of confident calm, gained access to the building.

It could have happened that way. Shame on you for thinking the worst.

Headlights appeared in her rear-view mirror. They flashed on and off full beam. It was Josh's powerful Porsche. He was signalling her to pull off the road. Right or wrong, she had no intention of obeying that signal. The Porsche swept past her, then pulled in dead ahead. He had slowed his speed to such an extent she was forced to follow suit. She had no choice. She couldn't detour around him. Clearly she had to pull over. He was intent on making that happen. She knew he wouldn't give up. The big problem was, she didn't feel like listening to his side of the story until her heart settled.

How perverse was that? Pronounce him guilty without giving him the opportunity to explain?

She pulled over onto the thickly grass carpeted verge, then switched off the engine, resting her head on the wheel of her car.

Pull yourself together. Don't let him know how shocked you are.

Self-admonished, she lifted her head, watching him as he stepped out of the Porsche. He loomed very tall and formidable. Nevertheless, an odd calm began to wash over her. She had her opportunity to have it out with him. Get to the bottom of things. All these unanswered questions with Josh were driving her mad.

She lowered the passenger window as he came to the side of her car. "Are you prepared to listen?" he asked, resting his elegant hands on top of the glass.

"You've got about two minutes before I deliver a verdict," she said.

"Is that so? Open the door, Clio. Or get out."

She was so stressed she laughed. "You might be tempted to slug me." Immediately she felt ashamed. "Joke, just a joke," she apologized, holding up a conciliatory hand. "Get in."

He did so, immediately pushing the passenger seat back to accommodate his long legs. "What were you doing anyway? Spying on me?" He looked across at her hard. "Push your seat back. I don't want to be talking to the side of your head."

"Okay, okay." She reached down to slide her seat back so it was in line with the passenger seat. Inside the car it was almost unbearably claustrophobic. She could feel the force of him, breathe in the clean male scent of him. That alone acted like an intoxicant. She didn't know if she had the strength to withstand this man. Yet she sustained a pretence. "I'm not *that* interested in you, Josh."

"You'd have fooled me, princess."

The sarcasm undercut her. "All right!" she retorted. "I wanted to be the first person to tell you Leo included you in his will. You'll be notified, of course, by the executor of Leo's will."

"Morgenstern, right?"

"Did you already know?" She stared at him. In the interior lights his eyes glittered like jewels.

His expression was enigmatic. He was so hard to read.

"I thought Leo would leave me some memento." He shrugged. "He hinted as much, but we all thought Leo was in better shape than he was. Leo and I never touched on the subject. Is that plain enough?"

Her mind slipped into another gear. "What a mess! So Keeley thought she had the ideal opportunity to pop over to tell you herself?"

"That's the polite way of putting it," he said very dryly. "Keeley popped over on the off chance she might get a bit of sex."

Who wouldn't want sex with Josh? she thought, swallowing with difficulty. "No need to be crude." Even to her own ears she sounded a prude.

"It's the conclusion *you* jumped to, isn't it?" he challenged, seeing the stain of colour mount under her beautiful skin. "Prim old you! Why didn't you get out of the car and come over if you were so interested in finding out what was going on?"

"Be glad I didn't," she said tightly. "But you let her up to the apartment. You must have."

"Did I really ever say you're highly intelligent?" he asked in a laconic voice.

"All right, she managed to slip past tenants going out?" She gave a brief laugh, more from relief than anything else.

"Now we've got *that* straight."

Anger flared again. "Why didn't you toss her off the balcony? You could have if you wanted to."

"That's right, Clio. I'm all about violence." It came out a lot harsher than he intended, but his self-control was coming under massive assault with the two of them in the car. He was almost crazy to pull her over into his lap. Take control.

She bowed her dark head. "I'm sorry, Josh. I confess to being overwrought. We've only just buried Leo. Keeley is bringing my father, indeed the whole Templeton family, down. You'll have to forgive me if I'm a little out of my mind."

"I have to take it as an excuse, then?" he asked.

Was it a trick of the soft lighting or was his expression unforgiving? She reacted at once. "I don't give a damn what you take," she said, her voice abruptly breaking. She had never ever been so close to Josh, let alone in such a confined space. She had been this close to him in her imagination, but this was for real. Josh was different from any other man she had ever known. The excitement was shattering. One should fear having one's composure totally dismantled. Her flesh tingled. There were tremors all over her body, tiny knife thrusts between her legs. She had read of such extreme sexual arousal. Now she was experiencing it.

"Could that be construed as a green light?" he challenged in a hard, bold voice.

She swung her head in surprise towards him, encountered that piercing blueness. "Josh, I—"

He, the control junky, couldn't control himself. Too many hungers were erupting. His yearning for this woman was pathetic. It split him wide open.

She didn't know quite how he did it, but he reached for her and drew her across the console and into his lap, cradling her like a child. She might have *been* a child, he did it with such ease.

"You're *two* people," she gasped.

"Shhh!" He cupped her beautiful delicate face

with his hand, his nostrils inhaling her fragrance. "Keeley wouldn't even rate beside you in the art of seduction." His voice dropped deep into his chest.

For once he didn't attempt to hide his expression. It was so exquisitely tender, so disarming, it brought tears to her eyes. She tried to hold them back, but they rolled out of her radiant dark eyes and down her cheeks.

"So now you cry?" His breath was on her cheek as he gathered up her teardrops with his tongue, carrying them most erotically into his mouth. "You cry for Leo. You cry for your father. You cry for yourself."

"I cry for *you*, Josh, whether you like it or not. You have so much hurt locked up inside you, but you won't let it out."

"Ah, Clio," he groaned. Her gaze on him was so steady she might have been trying to reach his soul. "You think if we sat down together and had a long talk, the demons that ride my shoulder would all fly off?" He spoke with some cynicism.

"Maybe we can get rid of them one by one. I know the past can never go away, Josh. Not for anyone. Not for me. We all have our memories, the good ones, the bad ones. The bad ones aren't easily forgotten. With you, the boy is still locked up inside the man. It might help if you could talk to me."

"Clio, your tears would run in rivulets." Clearly she had insight into his mind, but he wasn't ready to start unravelling. Not even with Clio. "I think my neuroses, if that's what you've diagnosed, would be way too much for you to handle."

"How would you *know* if you won't even allow me to ask a question? I can only guess at the severity of the damage that was done to you."

"So what question would that be?" he asked sardonically, trailing a finger down her cheek. "You almost swallowed an illicit affair between your stepmother and me."

She took a shuddery breath. Her body was in a state of agitation, her heart racing. "You're too much for me, Josh."

"I *know*," he said. "So what draws us together?"

"I can tell you *my* reason," Clio spoke with great fervour. "I *long* to know you better."

"You want me to reach out?"

He sounded as if he was determined to dissociate himself from that. "Well, why not, then?" she pleaded. "I sincerely believe sharing would help. I'm sorry if I had a split second of misjudging you, Josh. I should have known better."

"*I* think so," he said, putting a lot of feeling behind it. That Clio trusted him was all-important to him.

"So what are we doing here now?" she asked, with a rush of heartbeats.

"You're comfortable, aren't you?" He gave her a mocking smile.

"I don't know that *comfortable* is the right word," she said, not with her body on fire. "It's astonishing how you got me into this position. I feel like a doll."

"Not to *me* you don't," he said. "I'll let you go in a minute, Clio, but first let me tell you what draws me to *you*. It might even be better if I showed you." He shifted the weight of her slender body until she was lying back, her dark head resting against his shoulder. "You have such a lovely mouth," he murmured.

"Do you know you're the only man to make me fully conscious of my own beauty?"

"I like that." He bent his head towards her with a hungry yearning motion until their lips met.

Every atom of her being rose to meet him. Everything he did was beautiful to her. She abandoned herself to a state of euphoria, with no thought of denying him. Being with Josh was like breaking out of a cocoon. He could do what he liked with her. It was *that* bad.

For Josh it was rapture. To have all her sweetness, even as he knew it was a rapture that could tear him to pieces. Their fatal attraction had been forged many years before. The bond had never frayed or broken. But it could be just another sad tale of doomed love. At that moment it didn't matter. Nothing mattered but the taste and the touch of her mouth, the sweet flicker of her tongue as it mated with his. She was perfectly willing to allow him to explore her mouth, willing to allow him to push his hand into the neckline of her shimmering silk dress, his fingers slipping beneath the soft lace of her bra to trace a long slow curl around the dark pink aureole surrounding her aroused nipple. Her little helpless moans drove him on. His fingers moved in to take the tight bud between finger and thumb. He could hear the way her breathing had changed, deepened. Their desire for each other bridged all divisions. Her body was sinking inwards to him. She had to be aware of his powerful erection.

Smothering sensations were bearing down on them, wave after wave crashing onto cliffs with their inner tumult blocking out the roar. What they had felt for each other for so long demanded expression.

He continued to kiss her, strangely languid yet immensely passionate kisses that made the hot blood rip through his veins. They were outside time and place now. There was only obliterating excitement. His hands travelled down over the slight curve of her stomach, the tips of his long fingers reaching lower. He wanted to remove her every item of her clothing. He wanted to know every inch of her body. He wanted for her to know him. He wanted to open his whole *self* to her, what he had endured, but he didn't think he could bear her stricken face.

They had reached a point when Clio's breath was coming in unstable gulps. Nothing so life-changing, so confronting, had ever happened to her before. She was losing herself in him. Her dark head slumped forward.

"Clio?" He heard the worry in his voice. He had to stop. For a moment he hated himself for his loss of control. His endless desire for her was driving her too hard. Wasn't that what he feared?

"It's okay, Josh. I'm all right, just a little dizzy." Her voice was soft and whispery, the syllables a little slurred.

With exquisite gentleness he lifted her chin. "I don't know how to properly approach you, Clio."

"Oh, Josh." She was desperate to reassure him. "No one could ever approach me better."

"We were getting in too deep?" he asked. "You're bothered by being in the car?" Why wouldn't she be?

"Yes," she confirmed. "It has nothing to do with the fact someone might see us. It has more to do with my need to lie down. All the strength seems to have left my limbs."

"So, the right time, and the right place." Resolutely Josh drew her supple body back into a sitting position, supporting her against his shoulder. "Will that ever happen, do you suppose?" His voice was rough with emotion.

She didn't hesitate. "Wishes can come true, Josh."

"That's your answer?" He gave a laugh that held little humour. "What if I asked you out to dinner?"

Her throat rippled. "I'd like that."

"It seems to me it would have to be out of town, wouldn't it?" he replied sardonically. "Someone is always watching us, ready to spread the rumours. I should tell you I don't like you getting mixed up in the Crowleys' affairs. I understand Susan Crowley's problems but there are other law firms in town."

"She trusts me, Josh. And I'm another woman."

"I understand that too. But in coming to you she's exposing you to trouble. Think about it, Clio. Leo's death has in a sense left you defenceless. Your father isn't thinking straight. I've had old Paddy try to run interference in *my* business affairs."

"Have you?" she asked worriedly, twisting her head to look up at him.

"He'd do anything to hurt me. Leo was the buffer. Didn't you realize that? Crowley couldn't show his hand with Leo around. But Leo's gone, and with him a great deal of support. Paddy Crowley thinks it's only a matter of time before you marry his grandson. He's always had his eyes on the mansion, only he would pull it down and build some monstrosity or parcel the land and sell it off."

"That's *not* going to happen, Josh."

"Try telling Jimmy," he responded crisply. "These days you're on your own in that huge house, Clio. It bothers me greatly. I know you've got Meg and Tom—good people, but they couldn't handle anything. And they live in the grounds. Get them back in the house. At least for a while."

She turned her face into the hollow of his neck. "Are you trying to frighten me, Josh?"

"God, no," he said forcefully. "I'm trying to put you on your guard. Would you allow me to get the security system at the house upgraded? It's well past time. Home security systems have improved enormously, Clio. Apart from the house, it's filled with very valuable art, antiques, furnishings. You need high-tech burglar and fire protection. I know of an excellent firm."

She had considered upgrading security herself with Leo gone. Still she voiced a mild protest, "No one would hurt me."

"Of course not," he answered a little roughly, by no means sure about that and unwilling to take the chance. "I just want you safe."

"But *you* think the best way to keep me safe is steering clear of me." She angled her body so she could put one hand against his chest.

"What do you call *this*?" he asked, locking his two arms around her. "It might be a good idea if you got back in the driving seat."

"Give me a minute, can't you?"

"You can stay there for ever as far as I'm concerned."

"Why can't we sleep together, Josh?"

He took a moment to answer. "You mean you're prepared to totally abandon yourself to me? This man you hardly know? How is that possible?"

"Not possible unless you let me in, Josh. Take me inside you. Don't push me away."

"Like 'Open Sesame'," he said.

She could feel the tension rise in him like he was arming himself for attack. "Okay, stick to your cage," she said quietly, kissing him on the cheek. "I think its time for me to get behind the wheel, don't you?"

He shifted his legs, opened the door. He waited until she rounded the car and strapped herself into the driving seat. "You know you don't have to consider setting up business on your own, Clio. Buy the Crowleys out. You have the money. You don't need Vince or Jimmy. Let them set up shop elsewhere. You'll find far better lawyers to replace them. Speak to your father."

That triggered a dry laugh from her. "Dad won't go along with that, Josh."

"He really has no inkling of how the Crowleys operate?"

Clio sighed deeply. "You know as well as I do that the Crowleys are long established in this town. People kowtow to them. It's the same old story. Paddy has a lot of money. That buys him power and influence. Only one man he bowed to. Leo."

"There are ways of dealing with the Crowleys." Josh's expression turned hard.

"God, you're not going to start a gang war, are you?" It was only half a joke.

His blue eyes blazed. "Why does it always end up I'm the bad guy?"

"You overreact. You're a tough guy." She reached out a calming hand to stroke his cheek.

There was such warmth and tenderness in the gesture. It seemed extraordinary to him that she could care so deeply about him. "I'd go into battle for *you*, Clio," he said. "No one will ever try to harm you with me around."

"I've no doubt of that," she said, knowing it was true. Josh would never see her defenceless. "You might have to cross swords with Paddy and Vince," she said, "but Jimmy is a pushover."

The muscles along his clean jaw line tightened. "I can hand you a lever. Over the years I've made valuable contacts and gained a lot of inside information. Remember Chris Patterson—the builder that went bust some years back?"

Clio frowned, trying to recall the name. "Ah, yes, Vince handled his bankruptcy petition."

"Among others in the construction business." There was steel in Josh's voice. "Vince's clients paid very heavily for services they didn't get. Botched services they did get. It wouldn't be difficult to check out Vince's mistakes or maybe poor old Jimmy prepared the paperwork for him. Either way, both should pay. Patterson hates Crowley, but he still doesn't have the money to sue a partner in a highly regarded law firm like Templetons."

"You have proof?" Clio was deeply disturbed that the firm's core values might have been trashed.

"I wouldn't be saying so if I didn't."

Clio took a deep breath. "Okay, we move on Vince Crowley," she said.

CHAPTER FOUR

SHE had never driven with tears streaming down her face before. She had never been so humiliated, rejected, or made to feel like a tramp. Keeley dashed a hand across her eyes, smearing mascara down her cheeks. Damn it all, she would have to pull over. Fix her make-up. Get herself together before she returned home to her darling husband. At least Lyle had never turned to the grog. Nor would he dream of shouting at her, or abusing her in any way. Lyle Templeton, the perfect gentleman.

Josh Hart was the bad guy, the dangerous guy, the *hateful* guy. She knew which one she preferred. Somehow she would get even with Josh Hart. She had thought she was pretty good at reading the signals. Now, as it turned out, she was colour blind. Keeley pulled over, muttering to herself. Where the hell was her handbag? It had fallen off the passenger seat onto the floor. She reached for it, her head coming up just in time to see a silver Mercedes with Clio at the wheel, closely followed up by Josh Hart's Porsche speeding by. What the hell was this, a car chase? What were they doing? Where were the cops?

She heard herself shouting out loud.

Didn't you just know it? Josh and her step-daughter had become involved. She just knew it. Call it a woman's intuition. Especially a very jealous woman. Wouldn't her dear husband love confirmation of that? Triumph flared in her eyes.

See how easy it is, Keeley girl, to take revenge.

Her father's secretary, Helen Walters, stood in front of the door of his office, blocking the way. "Your father is busy, Clio," she said, apologetically, looking as though she was about to faint.

"That's okay, Helen." Clio smiled. "I'm going in. Please stand aside. I'll take full responsibility."

"Oh, Clio!" Helen Walters near wailed. "Your

father is in such a mood! I've never seen him like this in all my years."

"So you've warned me. Go back to your desk, Helen."

Helen went. Clio Templeton had an authority her father quite lacked.

Fury was written all over Lyle's face. "I told Helen I wasn't to be disturbed," he said severely. "What are you doing here, Clio?"

"I work here, Dad, remember?"

"I don't want to see you," he said, his furious expression not easing.

"You won't want to see this either."

"What?" Lyle's cold eyes flashed to the files in his daughter's hands.

"Enough to nail Vince Crowley," she said, slamming the papers down on her father's desk. "Force him out of our family firm. You know deep down he has no integrity, Dad. This proves it."

Lyle Templeton looked staggered. "I have no idea what you're talking about."

"That's the great pity of it, Dad," Clio said

gently. "You haven't been firing on all cylinders. So much easier to hide your head in the sand."

Lyle stood up. "I know about *you*," he said, tears stinging his eyes. "My beautiful daughter sleeping with a criminal."

Clio fought down s tremendous rush of anger. "How's that? I haven't slept with Jimmy Crowley. I'd say he was a criminal by default."

"You know who I'm talking about," Lyle persisted, doggedly.

"I'm not sleeping with anyone, Dad." Clio wearily shook her head. "You and Leo made it as difficult as you knew how. Think about it. The two of you would have been happy with a perennial virgin, only I had to provide Templeton heirs. You do *not* have control of my life. Both you and Leo seemed to think you had."

"Keeley *saw* you," he said, giving way to a shout.

"What, in bed?" she countered acidly. "You're going to believe Keeley, an inveterate liar?"

Lyle sat down again as though his legs wouldn't hold him up. "She thought it her duty to tell me.

She saw the two of you speeding away from his apartment."

"On surveillance, was she? Or just passing by?"

"God, Clio!" Lyle said in distress. "Are you in love with Josh Hart?"

Her feelings for Josh were way too private to share. "I'm not here to answer questions, Dad. But because it's you and I love you, I'll tell you I'm not sleeping with him. I promise. Even Josh thinks it's a bad idea," she added with irony. "You'd better wake up soon, Dad. Don't you think Mum would want you to? You have to deal with life. *I* want the Crowleys out. I want new people in. I want to get cracking on creating a scholarship program for our clever students who want to study law or whatever."

"Like Hart?" he asked bitterly. "He's veered off, hasn't he?"

"The fact he knows the law is a tremendous help to him," Clio pointed out. "Is it so difficult for you to speak to Keeley about a divorce?"

Her father winced. "I don't like the idea of divorce. No one has ever divorced in our family."

"There's always a first time and Leo isn't

around to tut-tut, not that he would in this case. Keeley doesn't love you. You don't love her. Stay with her and you'll descend totally into depression. Start divorce proceedings. Begin afresh."

Her father gave her a stony look. "Don't start on *me* when we're supposed to be talking about *you*. I won't have you mixing with the likes of Josh Hart."

"Leo let you down, didn't he, Dad?" Clio said sadly. "You saw him as always turning to Josh instead of you. But Leo loved us."

"Adored *you*. And your mother. I don't know about *me*." Lyle showed a lifetime of severely injured feelings.

"*I* love you."

"I know that," Lyle sighed.

"Then don't make this a personal vendetta. Josh Hart is very clever and very brave. He's come through terrible times in life. If he bashed up some minder, you can bet your life the guy deserved it. You simply can't run around calling him a criminal. It has to stop. You'd be showing a bit of courage yourself, taking on the Crowleys. We can buy them out. Let them take their clients. We don't need them. Everyone knows about Paddy, the old rogue. All I'm asking is you take a look at what Vince and Vince's monkey, poor Jimmy, have been up to. That would only be the tip of the iceberg. It all happened since Leo left the firm. You were supposed to be in charge."

Lyle flushed scarlet. "Clio, I've done the best I can."

Clio shook her head. "No, you haven't, Dad. You can do better and these files might give you a kick-start."

It was dead easy to spot the guy who was following him. He very nearly laughed. Watching his back had become part of him. He'd been expecting something of the sort. This punk was tall, around thirty, very fit, wearing jeans and a black T-shirt, black shades even though dusk was falling. Dark glasses or not, Josh knew the guy's eyes were glued to him. He wasn't worried whether he could take care of him. In all probability, old Paddy had organised the whole thing.

One positive thing had emerged. Lyle Templeton, with Clio's persuasion, had finally

AUSTRALIA'S MAVERICK MILLIONAIRE

found the guts to buy his partner out of the family firm. Crowley had gone, begging for no follow-up, and taking his "boofhead son" with him, along with their list of clients. Vince was given no guarantee the matter wouldn't go further. Victims were entitled to compensation.

The security company had gone to work at the Templeton mansion. The mansion had new electronic gates, cameras, motion detectors. Josh had really wanted a guard on the gate during the Crowley business but Clio had refused point blank. Leo had never bothered about security. Leo had lived through a time when it hadn't been needed. Anyway, Leo had felt himself way above threat from his subjects.

Times had changed.

The guy was still trailing him. Did he seriously think his antics were going unnoticed? This was getting tiresome. He turned down Florist Alley, which stretched away to a backstreet. If the guy was going to make a move, he was going to do it here. Dark alleyways were notorious for attack. The flower stalls at this time in the evening were emptied of produce. Not a single person hung around.

He strode ahead as if he didn't have a care in the world. All the while he was waiting for his psycho friend to approach. As it was, he had sensed the very instant the guy turned into the alleyway in silent pursuit. Probably intended to drop him like a stone then get in a few telling kicks to the kidneys and the groin. Old Paddy wouldn't be looking for another funeral. Just some heavy-handed tactics. It was a strategy that had worked for him in the past.

Josh awaited the precise moment to make his own move. He pivoted abruptly, throwing the guy off balance and getting a headlock on him with little effort. His would-be assailant, taken by surprise, was reduced to groaning and thrashing his hands about, shocked to find he was the one in powerful bother...

At about the same time that evening Clio encountered a problem of her own. She had stayed late to lessen her workload but the moment she stepped out of the office building and into the street, Jimmy Crowley raced towards her, looking as usual as harmless as a cocker spaniel.

"Clio, could you give me five minutes of your time?" There was a pleading note in his voice. "We're friends, aren't we?"

"Which doesn't mean I trust you, Jimmy," Clio informed him tartly. "Unfortunately for you, you're a Crowley."

"Ah, hell!" Jimmy groaned. "Don't give me the sins of the fathers bit. My grandfather isn't a man you cross. Did you ever try crossing *your* grandad?" he challenged. "Old bastards, both of them. Wouldn't you agree?"

Clio shook her dark head. "Come off it, Jimmy. Leo did a lot of good. He wasn't a white-collar criminal."

"But he *was* an old tyrant." Jimmy looked her right in the eyes. "Even Paddy wasn't game to be disrespectful. You weren't allowed to do your own thing. Not with Leo."

Clio made no attempt to deny it. These days she was deeply into self-analysis.

"We can have a cup of coffee," Jimmy suggested, sensing she was weakening. "What about Gino's?"

"No confrontations, Jimmy," Clio warned. It was hard to be mad at Jimmy. Basically he was just a simple guy.

"No." Jimmy's voice sounded so soft and helpless he might have been a child. "Are you really going to help Mum get a divorce?"

Anger suddenly flooded Clio's body. "Don't sons defend their mothers? Where the hell were *you*, Jimmy, when your father was browbeating your mother?"

"Under the bed," Jimmy said without hesitation. "Don't think I'm not ashamed of myself. A guy like Josh Hart would have hammered Dad to the ground even if Dad was coming at him with a machete. I'm not brave like that, Clio. My dad and old Paddy make me sick to my stomach."

"Okay, it was hard for you," Clio acknowledged, knowing Jimmy hadn't been spared Vince's vicious tongue and temper. "Look, have you had anything to eat?" Jimmy, always gym trim, appeared to have lost six or seven kilos. The weight loss didn't suit him.

"Find it hard to eat these days." Jimmy gave her a wan grin.

"Let's go home," Clio came to a decision. "Meg will fix us something."

Jimmy brightened. "If it comes to court, I'll testify for Mum. After that, I'll have to beat it out of town. Who tipped you off about the bankruptcy petitions? My stupid fault. Not Dad's. I pulled a lot of wrong credit information."

"I know, Jimmy. Why don't you check out another career while you're on the run? I'm sure you'll get your mother to go with you. She loves you. She doesn't blame you for anything."

"She's a saint, I swear," Jimmy proclaimed.

Less than twenty minutes later, with matters settled entirely to his satisfaction and with no need whatsoever for violence, Josh returned to his car, calling up his messages. His eye lit on one that caused him to give a bitter smile. Only one person it could be: Keeley Templeton. This was a woman who got around.

Guess who's up at the house with your girlfriend? Jimmy Crowley. If you doubt me go see. Jimmy always does what he's told. What do you know about Clio's relationship with Crowley anyway? She likes the guy.

For all Jimmy was a Crowley, he didn't see him being a threat to Clio. Jimmy worshipped her. Still, what was he doing at the house? He thought he had made it clear Clio should be on her guard against the Crowleys. After the failed attack tonight, Kingpin Paddy Crowley's day was fast coming to an end.

The massive wrought-iron gates had been fitted with a keypad plus remote-control entry for family. He wasn't family—he was rootless wasn't he, no background? he thought ironically, but for him his relationship with Clio had entered a staggering new dimension. It was almost dreamlike. To have held Clio in his arms. To have kissed her passionately when he had spent years obliged to keep a respectful distance. He couldn't seem to grasp it. No matter his success in life, he had to conclude the past had damaged him. One didn't need a degree in psychology to figure that out.

Most people, and certainly the privileged, knew nothing about institutionalized life and how it created long-term problems. The abandoned were at high risk. He knew of deaths on the streets of the kids he had once known.

It surprised him when Clio activated the gates. He had expected Tom, who had acted as Leo's major-domo. She didn't mention Jimmy Crowley was with her. For that matter, *was* he? Or was Keeley having a little bit of fun, keeping Clio and him under constant scrutiny?

Jimmy's car wasn't parked in the drive. Too late to turn back. Clio, with her beautiful hair cascading down her back, was standing at the door by the time he made it up the short flight of steps. "Is anything the matter, Josh?" She looked her surprise, waving him in.

"So far, so good." His eyes swept her. She had changed out of her office clothes into an ankle-length floaty dress with shoestring straps. Jimmy would have loved it. "I was passing so I thought I might check in. You're not having any problems?"

She gave him a smile. "I feel very safe, Josh, thanks to you."

"Where's Meg?" He looked around as they walked down the entrance hall with its beautiful honey-coloured polished timber floor and a custom-made runner in muted blues, reds and golds, exquisite in detail. The informal dining room was to the left where Clio was heading.

"She prepared a light meal then went off to the bungalow to join Tom."

"I thought they were staying in the house for a while," he commented, thinking he too was getting over-protective. Clio had that effect on the men in her life.

"Josh, I'm living in Fort Knox. Cameras, motion detectors, back-up systems, panic buttons."

"There's you, and you have a great deal to protect," he pointed out. "I know you don't like using the word 'mansion' in connection with the house, but that's what this place is. It's a load off my mind to know you're now living in a secure house, as you should be."

"I stand corrected." She gave a gracious bob of her glossy head. "And it makes me happy to know you care. Come through, Josh. Jimmy Crowley is here."

Without thinking, he bit out, "What the hell for?"

"I *invited* him," Clio said sweetly, with a lift of her chin.

"I see. He's going to propose if it's the last thing he ever does?"

She shook her head at his caustic humour. "Look, I feel affection for poor Jimmy, okay? He's really a gentle person."

"And I'm not?"

She spun around to face him. Her olive skin shimmered, her face, her slender arms, her beautiful bare shoulders. "God knows, you *need* gentling," she said very softly.

Despite her words, the note in her voice made him feel like she had kissed him on the mouth. "What did he do with the Bentley?" he asked, trying to tamp down the mad rush of desire. "Run it into the garage under cover?"

"Actually, you could do me a huge favour and run Jimmy back into town when you leave. I brought him here in the Merc."

"For a tête-à-tête?"

"Jimmy is harmless. That's all I care about."

"So what do we have here, overnight liberation?'

"What, for Jimmy or for me?" Her lustrous eyes were huge in her face, dark enough to be near black, yet brilliant.

"*Your* safety is all I care about. But it takes guts to cross a tyrant. I wonder if Jimmy's got them?"

She glanced over her shoulder. "I haven't actually seen that much of his body, Josh. We're out on the terrace. Would you care for a drink? There's still plenty of food."

"Thank you, I'm fine. I had a couple of beers at the pub with one of Paddy Crowley's splendid part-time workforce, the paid head-kickers. I'll say hello to Jimmy. He might be interested to know his grandad mightn't be the big man he once was."

"And *you're* going to take over?" She felt a spurt of anxiety. Josh downing beers in the pub with one of Paddy Crowley's bouncers? It was critical, Leo had always maintained, that Josh stay out of trouble.

He gave her a searing look. "You can't stop yourself, can you?"

"I need to work on it," she admitted wryly. "Please tell me how to go about it."

His expression was back to imperious mode. "Figure it out for yourself."

Clio turned away. "I will. I owe you."

Josh was a puzzle she might never understand but no matter what amount of persuasion from him she was going to win him over.

Jimmy sat as if paralysed, then nearly desperately shot to his feet as Clio, with Josh looming tall at her shoulder, walked out onto the loggia.

Josh Hart? Jimmy thought in shock. Hart had been Leo's protégé but to his knowledge Hart had never been encouraged to call in on Clio. That old tyrant, Leo, would have actively discouraged it. Any man that courted Clio had to be a member of a family of power and influence. Most people had been baffled by Leo Templeton's close involvement with Josh Hart.

It was easy for Josh to read Jimmy's mind. He looked around, brushing away any thought of resentment. The loggia was the perfect setting for outdoor relaxing and entertaining. His eyes moved swiftly over the glass-topped circular dining table beautifully set for two. Candles, hibiscus flowers, a bottle of wine in a silver cooler. Quite romantic really. And Jimmy was seriously romantic about Clio. Professional lighting had been installed to bring the lush gardens and the pool area to life. Indigo blue and aqua mosaic tiles lined the swimming pool and the spa. A glorious display of bougainvillea wreathed many of the stone-arched columns that formed the colonnade. All in all as much as anyone could possibly want.

All at once Josh felt a ferocious sadness for the kid he had been. No home life at all. Nothing normal. The reverse. No loving parents to guide his way. Plenty who had wanted him restrained. He could buy all this, the Templeton mansion, but he was beginning to doubt if he could ever find his way out of the wasteland that was his past. He sometimes thought of it as a kind of stigma attached to him.

"Josh, how are you?" Jimmy, with heightened colour, thrust out his hand.

"Thank you for asking," Josh said suavely, responding to the handshake. Jimmy had always avoided him like the plague.

"Sit down, Josh, won't you?" Clio invited, a near plea-like note in her voice.

"Glad to." He pulled up a chair from an adjacent setting, remaining standing while he held Clio's chair. "So, Jimmy, what have you been up to since your shock departure from Templetons?" he asked conversationally.

"Josh!" Clio hurriedly intervened, while Jimmy looked too startled to answer.

"I had a word with one of your grandfather's bouncers this evening," Josh revealed conversationally.

"Really? Which one?" Jimmy asked fearfully.

"A guy called Bruiser O'Malley. You know him?" There was no threat or anger in Josh's voice but it managed to thoroughly chill Jimmy.

Jimmy did know O'Malley. "Why should the sins of my grandfather come down on *my* head?" he groaned.

"Tough, I know." Josh sounded like he understood. "You need to get a life, Jimmy. I'd say without delay. I know you worship the ground

Clio walks on, but that's not going anywhere, is it?"

Clio broke in. "Excuse me, Josh, but has it escaped your attention I'm still here?"

He turned to her. "Forgive me, Clio. It was more like my trying to help Jimmy. We both know he has to sort himself out quickly. Don't you, Jimmy?" He pinned Paddy Crowley's grandson with his piercing gaze.

"And how do I do that?" Jimmy cried, like a man desperately in need of advice. "It's a little late for me to morph into Iron Man, like you. Did you knock O'Malley's block off?" he asked with a certain relish.

"Actually, O'Malley had the great good sense to send someone else. I have the whole pathetic plan down on paper. Signed, witnessed. O'Malley thinks he's my new best friend."

Jimmy took a deep breath. "Well, *I* wouldn't care to make an enemy of you," he said.

Clio ignored Jimmy. "What happened, Josh?" All sorts of anxieties were crowding in. "Are the police going to arrive on my doorstep?"

Josh stared at her. "What?'

"I'm worried about you," she said. "Can't you understand that? Paddy Crowley is a psycho. Isn't he, Jimmy?"

"I've had a lifetime to find out," said Jimmy. "Take my old man—"

"Was there a fight, Josh?" Clio didn't want to hear about Jimmy's old man.

"Not yet anyway," Josh said with a decided edge to his voice. "I don't have to account to you, Clio," he said, with a sudden mood swing.

Hot colour rose to her cheeks. "Josh, I'm someone you can *trust*."

"*You* don't trust *me*," Josh said pointedly. He rose to his splendid height, shoving his chair with a loud scrape into the table. "No trust. No friendship." It sounded like an ultimatum, stripped down to the bone.

"Listen, Clio didn't mean anything." Jimmy attempted appeasement, thoroughly intimidated by Josh's sheer size.

"Of course she did." Josh swept Jimmy's excuse aside. "I'm the obligatory bad guy in town. Every town has to have one." Josh turned his blazing gaze on Jimmy. "Do you want a ride back into town?"

Jimmy looked like he very much feared to decline. "If it's no trouble, Josh. I don't have my car."

"Trade it in," Josh advised.

"It doesn't belong to me anyway," Jimmy confided. "Dad leases our cars."

Clio made a grab for Josh's arm, feeling the taut muscles clench. "What's going on here, Josh?"

"Why, Clio, you're manhandling me." He stared down at her detaining hand. "I'll stop short of calling the police."

She stared at him, well aware of those dark places in Josh. Hate for the system that had failed him. Being a virtual prisoner through his formative years had left Josh with a legacy of pain and repressed fury. But despite everything he had managed to beat the odds. Nevertheless, there was still aggression in him, no matter how tightly he controlled it. She was fearful of him tangling with the Crowleys. Paddy Crowley made her skin crawl. No one made an enemy out of Crowley without paying a heavy price. "I've made you angry, haven't I?" she said, her dark eyes moving over his taut face.

He answered at once. "You *love* it, Clio."

"At least I can get *some* emotion out of you." A ridiculous statement, considering the emotions he could unleash in her at will.

"I don't think we need to go there. Come along, Jimmy. I'll go ahead so you can say your good-nights."

"Don't you walk away from me, Josh." Her voice spiked. His manner was unbearably autocratic. This was *her* house.

He made a sound, halfway between a laugh and a groan. He turned back to her, blue eyes blazing. Powerful emotions emanated from him, bewilderingly complex. With one swift movement he pulled her to him one-armed. His spread hand almost covered her slender, arched back. "'Night, Clio," he said tauntingly. "Sleep well."

Clio managed a muffled exclamation, as though expecting him to turn nuclear within seconds. The tension between them was phenomenal. She had the odd sensation she was falling.

Before his kiss came, she felt it. The effect was

immediate and total. It was a hard, punishing, thrillingly voluptuous kiss. Excitement flooded her body, followed by a perverse sense of shame, even womanly rage that he could so easily call up this frantic response in her. Damn him. Damn him!

Jimmy had to clutch the back of his chair for support while shock waves broke over him, nearly knocking him to his knees. God, Hart had just kissed Clio as though he *owned* her. It was a moment so intimate, so full of raw passion Jimmy felt he shouldn't be watching it.

CHAPTER FIVE

KEELEY TEMPLETON moved through the Templeton law offices like an express train. Her husband had taken an early flight to the state capital. He had left her a note on the refrigerator, of all places.

Meeting up with one of our most valued clients in Brisbane. Not sure when I'll be returning.

A scrawled L and some squiggles. Whatever had happened to proper writing? The more educated the person, the worse the writing. Hers, thankfully, was perfectly legible. She snatched it furiously, ripping the note into tiny pieces and flinging it around like confetti. Let the cleaning woman pick the pieces up and throw them in the bin. She and Lyle had had a furious argument the night before. Well, *she'd* been the furious one. True to form he had played the po-faced lawyer. She had known he wanted out but she still found it astounding. *He* wanted to get rid of *her*! It was outrageous. He'd never have found the guts to make a move only for that interfering little bitch, his daughter. The most sickening thing was the hunch that Clio's involvement with Josh Hart was escalating, however much they tried to hide it. Only there was no Leo any more to stand like a bulwark between them.

Clio and Josh Hart!

Just what the town needed! Princess Clio and a guy well and truly from the wrong side of the tracks. Lyle, like his father, was dead against it. The town would take sides. Well, she knew what side she was on! The same side she'd always been on.

Her own.

Clio's assistant, Peter Sommerville, knew the instant he set eyes on Mrs Templeton that there were going to be fireworks. Clio's door was open, making it easy for him to bring in files, like an overwhelming tide, so she could make herself familiar with a wider range of firm business. Losing that poisonous, pompous prat Vince Crowley had lightened up the office atmosphere to no end. Mr Templeton still kept to the old master/employee dynamic, but Clio had an outstanding talent for getting on with everyone.

Peter strode down the corridor, thinking how best to protect her. One couldn't exactly whip an apprehended violence order under the nose of a formidable Mrs Templeton—no way a *lady*—on the warpath.

"Mrs Templeton, may I help you?" Peter called with urgency, envisioning how she might turn on him. He'd heard a few hair-raising tales about Keeley Templeton before her advantageous marriage.

Clio, hearing Peter's upraised voice, came to the open door, her expression calm. "Keeley, come in." She looked beyond her stepmother, ordering coffee as though this was a routine courtesy call.

Peter hurried away to find Ellie Sharp, one of the junior secretaries. In her own time Ellie wore a silver stud in her nose and several piercings elsewhere. She even had the boxing kangaroo tattooed at the base of her spine. He saw it whenever her T-shirts rode up.

Keeley charged into the office as if it were a prize fight arena instead of an office. "What is it this time, Keeley?" Clio asked.

Keeley responded savagely. "Your father has gone to Brisbane, did you know that?'

"Of course. We all know. Didn't you?"

"I damned well didn't," Keeley snapped. "We had a fight. Your father wants a divorce."

"About time, wouldn't you say, Keeley? Please sit down." Clio walked around her desk to resume her chair. "The marriage hasn't been a happy one."

"Because your father is a head case." Keeley was inhaling and exhaling deeply in her fury. "He's still in love with a dead woman."

"Of course he is," Clio agreed with faint melancholy. "We can't change the way we are. Seven years isn't all that long to grieve, is it? They say the older we get, the harder it is. I'd feel for you if you'd ever had any genuine affection for Dad. But you weren't bitten by the *love* bug, Keeley. It was the *money* bug."

Keeley threw back her head and laughed. "Congrats! Please don't tell anybody else."

"No need. Everyone knows. I take it you're looking for some kind of confrontation?"

"The whole point of coming here," Keeley confirmed.

"Then tell me and please don't raise your voice. I don't want to have to ask you to leave."

"Oh, boy!" Keeley jeered. "Haven't *you* grown inches! You'll be six foot in no time."

"It might help you to remember that. Why exactly are you here?"

There was a furious light in Keeley's hazel eyes. She felt like jumping up and slapping her stepdaughter hard. Instead, she saw wisdom and modified her tone. "It was *you* who talked your father into it. He's never had the guts before."

"I wouldn't call it guts, precisely," Clio said. "Dad didn't believe in divorce. I may have been instrumental in helping him come round."

"You bet you did! I'm going to clean him out, you know."

Clio stared back at her stepmother. "You wish! You'll be handsomely compensated, but I have read the pre-nup, Keeley. Leo knew this was going to happen one day. He never believed you fell pregnant before the marriage."

"Sure. It suited him to doubt me. He never liked me. Thought I was a real bimbo."

It was true Leo had not been kind to Keeley. Courteous. Not kind. "Keeley, you and Dad are both better off apart. There are no children to cause major concerns. You'll have money. You can move on. Start a new life."

Keeley's face suddenly lit up. "I know just the guy I'd like to share it with."

"Well, you've known plenty of guys in the past."

"Yeah? No one like Josh Hart!" Keeley crowed. "He's *dynamite*! The charisma, you can't escape it. He might be a real complex guy—he's sure not one to encourage friendships—but I've never struck anyone near as good in bed."

Clio regarded her stepmother coolly. "Get real,

Keeley. We both know you've never had sex with Josh Hart."

Keeley's smirked. "Told you that, did he?" She brought up a hand to smooth her newly groomed hair. "Men are such liars. I bet most of them are still lying on their deathbeds."

"Let's get off the subject of Josh Hart."

"You're hot for him, aren't you?" Keeley narrowed her eyes. "Not that I blame you. It makes me jealous. It even makes me a little crazy. Josh does that to women. But better to go a little crazy over a guy than never know what's it like. Josh has had a dozen affairs *I* know about. I could provide you with some very interesting information about him. He's violent, you know. He's even put the wind up Paddy Crowley."

"So you heard that? Good!" Clio held up her hand as a knock came on her door. She called, "Come in," and a moment later Ellie Sharp, whose brain matched her name, wheeled a trolley into the room. The rich aroma of freshly brewed espresso coffee permeated the air.

"Thank you, Ellie." Clio gave the girl a smile. She liked Ellie. A very positive young lady of unusual intelligence. Could do with a bit of help with her dressing.

Ellie returned the smile, shyly for her, then shifted her cropped raven head to look Keeley over. "Shall I pour?" she asked Clio, still keeping her remarkable green cat's eyes on Keeley.

"No, that's fine, Ellie."

"Right, then." Ellie gave Keeley another straight look.

Keeley waited until the girl had shut the door before turning back to Clio in amazement. "Who *is* that creature? Eyeing *me* off! The cheek of her! She should be sacked. And what sort of an ensemble has she got on? She looks like a hooker."

"Ellie favours black," Clio offered lightly. Ellie was wearing her everyday uniform—black blouse, short black skirt, black stockings even in the heat, Doc Martens or something very much like them on her small feet. Ellie was on probation but she had already proved she was way too smart for the job and had considerable computer skills. Clio had been playing around with the idea of offering Ellie Sharp a full scholarship to go to university. The Templeton family had always had a social conscience. She wanted to up the ante.

Clio poured the coffee. Keeley took a sip, frowned as though the brew wasn't up to her high standards. "There's a rumour Josh assaulted one of his girlfriends but it was all hushed up. Poor thing was probably too frightened to bring charges."

Clio felt the surge of blood to her face. "I'd be happy to bring a few charges against you, Keeley. You can't go around making damning allegations."

"Gee, I wouldn't think of it." Keeley was out to rattle her stepdaughter any way she could.

"Give me a name and I'll run a check. Or is it back to *she said, he said*?"

Keeley was backpedalling now. "You'd have to dig deep. And don't go around accusing me of anything. I'm trying to protect you as an older, wiser woman. Your father told me Josh had beaten up a minder or a foster-parent in the past. One or the other. You talk about making accusations! Your father put the rumour around Josh had something to do with Leo's fatal heart attack. Pot calling the kettle black? There are sordid things in Josh's past," Keeley maintained, knowingly.

Clio tried to remain calm. "On his own admission, Josh grew up with violence. It's a tragic fact of life that people in positions of responsibility regularly prey on the most vulnerable in society—the young, the old, the sick, the disabled, physically and mentally. Anyone who is vulnerable to attack. There are the good guys and the bad guys, but I'm happy to think the good guys are still in front. I choose to believe Josh was driven to defend himself from further assault."

"I bet there were other episodes," Keeley warned darkly, in reality turned on by Josh Hart's splendid male *toughness*. "We've all seen how fit Josh is. I hear he has a black belt in karate."

"Keeley, Josh *Hart* has lived in this town since he was thirteen years old. There's no disputing he was very difficult then, trying to flout authority at every turn, but once my grandfather got himself involved Josh calmed down appreciably. Leo was out to save him and save him he did. Josh enjoys an excellent reputation as a citizen and businessman. There is *no* record whatever of him having causing anyone any physical injury. In fact, he's held in high regard in the wider community."

"Just don't forget the carer," Keeley said like a mantra. "There are quite a few in this town who won't go within a foot of him. He radiates—"

"Authority," Clio cut in. "Sounds like Josh put you straight and you're mad about it. Hell hath no fury, etcetera."

Keeley flushed. "You've got it wrong. Josh sure breaks the tedium of living with your father."

"So the divorce shouldn't be a problem, then," Clio said briskly. "You'll get your money. Start afresh."

Moments later, Keeley stormed out of Clio's office, missing the Goth creature's "Cheers!" The meeting had not gone as planned. Time to formulate another strategy. She wasn't such a fool that she didn't know she had no chance with Josh. She had gone to his apartment that night thinking she might have a chance at seducing him, but he had warded her off as if she were a female vampire. She was dammed if she was going to let him fall under Princess Clio's spell. She never had suffered much remorse for any damage she had done in her life. Maybe she was devoid of the finer feelings?

Clio had to chase Josh to his car. Not all that easy in high heels. A few weeks ago she would have thought it madness. She was known to everyone in town. She was supposed to be a highly responsible and thus conservative lawyer. But how could that be? She was chasing Josh Hart and she wasn't about to give up. Anyway, who said lawyers were sane? The arrogant son of a gun had seen her, but it was obvious he was going to ignore her. Only she had to apologize to him for seeming to doubt him, even implying in a mad moment he might have drawn the police to her door. No excuses about being intensely worried about him, which she had been. That wouldn't work. And it had to be said she wasn't absolutely *certain* Josh wouldn't resort to violence if he felt the situation demanded it. There was rage in him. She knew it and understood it. Josh had experienced things she knew nothing whatever about.

Heads in the street were turning as she dashed after him. All showed amazement. She caught up as he was climbing behind the wheel. Nearly breathless, she opened the passenger door and threw herself in.

"Thanks a lot!" She blew out a gasping breath.

"I could have locked you out," he retorted quite calmly.

She could have socked him. "So why didn't you?" She looked him full in his drop-dead handsome face. No show of emotion there.

"I really don't know."

"Okay, we have a problem," she admitted.

"*You* have the problem, Clio," he said. "I did advise you to stay away from me."

"Well, I'm not going to do that, Josh," she told him sharply. "What's with you anyway? One minute you're warning me off, the next you're hauling me into your arms and kissing me senseless. How dare you do that? You're so madly contrary. It's like I said, you're *two* people."

For the first time his expression relaxed into his beautiful smile. "Take my word for it, I *am*. The torment of it! I can't bear to be with you. I can't bear to be away from you. In many ways it's like playing with fire."

"Please let me speak, Josh. I want to—I need to apologize to you for some of the things I said the other night."

He turned his head, his blue eyes sizzling over her. She was wearing a lovely sunshine-yellow dress with a wide black patent leather belt that showed off her tiny waist. It was an outfit both elegant and sexy. "What exactly *did* you say? I've forgotten."

"Of course you haven't," she retorted impatiently. "Can you blame me for worrying about you when you tangle with Paddy Crowley's unholy bunch of bouncers?"

"Does tangling mean having a chat?" he asked suavely.

"Chat? I thought one of them tried to attack you?"

Josh shrugged a careless wide shoulder. "He wasn't very professional. Look, Clio, I appreciate your concern, but I've been looking after myself for a very long time. I've *tangled,* as you put it, with far worse characters than Paddy Crowley and, what was it, his unholy bunch of bouncers? I couldn't have said it better myself. But you know *nothing* about that side of life."

"Then I have much to be grateful for," she said with a faint shudder. "But I do know *this*. I care very much about you, Josh. You appear to be finding that disturbing. Is it a responsibility you don't need, or think you don't need? Either way, you can't talk me out of it. We forged an unbreakable bond that day you dived into Paradise Lagoon to save Ella. She was asking about you only last week. We all cling to that bond, Josh. You were our hero."

He gave a brief laugh. "You just might be able to claim that about Lisa and her family, but it didn't make your father any more friendly towards me. He's heaped all sorts of names on my head. C-r-i-m-i-n-a-l, for instance." Josh measured out the word.

Clio bowed her head and stared at her bare knees. Her short skirt showed a lot of leg. "I've talked to you about that. Dad felt Leo had more time for you than him. That would have hurt any son. You have to consider Dad's feelings."

"I have considered them, Clio, except your father's response to me is paranoid. He would never accept me as your friend, God forbid as a lover. I understand you wouldn't like me to criticize your father or Leo, but I'm pretty sure both of them would come under the category of elitists."

"Okay, you're probably right."

"Probably?"

She grabbed his arm tightly. "All right, elitists. Why don't you stop there? Leo got something right. He took on a trusteeship on your behalf."

"Sure he did," Josh freely admitted. "Clearly saving little Ella had a lot to do with it, otherwise I'd have been written off as a delinquent. Anyway, I thanked Leo many times over. I even made *more* money for him. I know had I done anything to discredit him I would have landed back in serious trouble."

He was right about that. "Whatever you say about my family, Josh—"

"Does that include Jezebel Keeley?" he asked suavely.

Clio's heart lurched. She was still recovering

from Keeley's surprise visit. "Please, God, she and Dad will divorce."

"I'm sure that's the best outcome," he said smoothly. "I know it's not in the best of taste but could I ask how in hell your father married her in the first place?"

"What does it matter now?" Clio sighed. "Are you going to accept my apology or not?"

His wide brow knotted. "You have to give me a chance to think about it."

She clenched her small fists in her lap. "Well, you'd better think *fast* because I'm out!"

His bluer-than-blue eyes rested on her highly expressive face. "Clio, Clio, you need to lighten up."

Her heart was racing. "That's *good*, coming from you. You can't even produce a smile."

"No one's perfect," he said.

Clio couldn't resist it. She punched him in the shoulder.

He caught her hand, carried it to his mouth. "Now, wasn't that a *good* feeling, Clio? Even you have a violent streak."

"I didn't have one until recently," she said tartly.

"And it's all about *you*. I've never punched anyone before. I'm a fervent advocate of non-violence."

He released her trembling hand. "I don't know if I believe you, Clio." With a mock grimace, he began rubbing his shoulder. "Do you want to have dinner tonight?"

That shocked her into silence. Even staring at him, she didn't know if he was serious or not. "Where?" she asked eventually, sitting trans-fixed.

"My place." He reached out to stroke her luminous cheek with its bright shimmer of blush. "You weren't able to get in the last time, remember?"

"On that occasion I was trying to be helpful." She put her hand over his. Just a touch yet her centre of gravity shifted. "May I bring someone?" She tried a joke when hot prickles of excitement rolled up and down her spine.

"No. Just you. Up for it?" He was watching her closely, as if she was being put to the test.

"I was serious, Josh, when I said you're my hero from way back."

"I'm talking about *now*," he responded, a shade tersely.

She looked down at her lap again. "You might terrify me, Josh, from time to time, but I trust you. Will you be kissing me?"

He eased back in the driver's seat. "Good God, no! Not in the main street with so many people passing by and staring avidly."

"It didn't bother you, kissing me in front of Jimmy Crowley?" she flared.

"A good reason there. Crowley has to drop any idea of winning the hand of the most beautiful girl in the world."

She felt real heat in her cheeks. "Don't be ridiculous. I'm not the most beautiful girl in the world or anything like it."

"Jimmy and I know differently," he said.

"Sounds like you're both biased. Anyway, I didn't mean kissing me *now* in the car, which you very well know. I meant what you have in mind for tonight, always supposing I say yes."

He smiled at her, sending all her defences flying. Then he spoilt it. "Well, I'm not asking you to move in," he drawled sardonically.

Clio's dark eyes flashed. "It wouldn't do you any good if you did." Her voice was icy. "I won't keep you a moment longer." She opened the door, then slid swiftly out of the passenger seat.

Josh lowered his head to call after her. "Seven o'clock suit to pick you up?"

Clio slammed the door hard, such a sparkle of mixed emotions on her face two dear old ladies of the town, approaching, gave her a little wave, but a wide berth. "Fine," she said.

Josh watched her move off with such spirit on her lovely long legs, then he put back his head and gave a laugh of pure, uncomplicated joy.

Joy?

He had thought he had lost it for ever.

CHAPTER SIX

IT WASN'T until the lift had taken them up to the penthouse that Clio posed the burning question. "How far did my stepmother actually get?"

"What do you mean—how far did she get?"

She recognised the daunting look down his straight nose. "Just interested." She shrugged her shoulders lightly.

"She didn't get very far at all. I met with her trying to get up while I was going down. I wasn't exactly angry, I was disgusted."

"Quite rightly."

"So I escorted her to the ground floor."

"Then walked her companionably to the door, but decided not to see her to her car."

"Well, you were sitting right across the street, watching it happen," he pointed out, moving across the carpeted corridor to his door. "Are you going to ease off now?"

"Yes, of course I am." Clio looked around her. "I feel honoured that you asked me to your classy abode. Could you please tell me why it has taken so long?"

He stood back to allow her entry, his nostrils tantalized by her lovely perfume. "You know perfectly well Leo didn't want me to ask you here."

Momentarily dazzled by the double-height living area that flowed seamlessly onto the broad terrace, Clio turned abruptly. "That's a bit strong, isn't it?"

Josh moved to the panel that controlled the lighting in all its different modes. "Wake up, sleeping princess. Leo put a lot of effort into seeing the initial bonding went no further. We had to function independently."

She had no good answer to that. She felt terribly conflicted. "But Leo loved you!"

Josh shook his head. "Something about me appealed to Leo's nature. I reminded him of the young man he was. I'm impelled to succeed. So was he. He could have sat on the money like your father, but he built greatly on the family fortune. He admired some quality in me. Our minds met at many levels. But Leo thought he *owned* me as well as you. I suspect he feared the day would come when he wouldn't."

"But he left you Aquarius. Money?" Surely that alone would take away all suspicion Josh and her grandfather had argued that fatal night. Or would it? Leo's will had already been made.

"Aquarius was *his* island, Clio," Josh said crisply, as though he was reading her mind. "Leo knew I could handle the kind of project he had in mind. Architect to the Pharoah, as it were. It was to be *Leo's* memorial."

She sought a sofa. Sank into its plush depths. "God, Josh, that's the way you think of it?"

"Don't you see it yourself?" he asked bluntly, choosing the sofa opposite. She was wearing a colour, a soft orange, in a gossamer fabric many women would have found difficult, but it suited her Mediterranean colouring beautifully. No other young woman could challenge her. She remained his ideal. His voice in no way betrayed the freight of hurt and humiliation he had felt for all the generosity Leo had heaped on him. "Leo kept us moving in different directions. You had to be guarded from the likes of me. He knew I wasn't someone he could always control. Leo *was* a control freak."

His words had a heavy impact. Since she had lost Leo, she had been forced to confront that knowledge.

"That's why he didn't mind Jimmy Crowley hanging about. Jimmy's a good-looking guy. He's not totally stupid. He would have done until someone Leo deemed suitable came along."

"Like I wasn't allowed to have a choice?" Clio asked with disillusionment. She was seeing her past life very differently now.

"Certainly not me," Josh said, meeting her eyes. "He believed in bloodlines and all that. Who knew what defects were in my genes? My father had to be despicable, leaving my mother young and pregnant. She didn't have the strength to survive. She was a fragile person. I wasn't, even though I was booted from pillar to post. You, on the other hand, have led a privileged life."

"Are you going to condemn me for that?" she asked.

"I don't condemn you, Clio. I don't envy you either."

Everything in her wanted to address the question, like a physician trying to make the right diagnosis. "You say your father must have been a despicable person, Josh, but you know *nothing* about him? It's even possible he knew nothing about *you*."

He grimaced. "I know you want to help me, Clio, as much as possible, but this isn't helping. My mother never said a word about the man who fathered me. So leave it, please. I despise him. We all have dark places in our souls. Unfortunately I have more than most." It would be much safer for her to be free of him, he thought. He still suffered short periods of intense misery, the lacerating flashbacks, the memories of brutality. No one knew better than he that people in positions of trust were not always trustworthy.

"There are always ways of finding things out, Josh," Clio persisted. "You told Leo you remembered your mother as being a small person with beautiful long dark hair."

He was on guard at once. "So Leo shared that with you, did he?"

"Don't be like that, Josh," she pleaded. "We're friends. That means—"

"I *know* what it means, Clio," he clipped out, addressing his own big issue. "You don't still suspect Leo and I had some sort of argument that brought on his heart attack?" He pinned her gaze.

She shook her head. "My heart tells me no."

"What does your *head* have to say?" he retorted bluntly.

For a moment there was no response from her. Was that an answer?

"*Tell* me," he insisted, plunged into a kind of despair.

He looked so formidable she could hardly get out the words. "My head says no as well, Josh." She knew she had to tread very carefully. "Leo left you the island."

"Which isn't all that much of an answer," he

responded. "Leo's will was already made, as you know."

She couldn't bear to have any yawning gulf between them. She changed the subject. "I'd love you to take me to the island in your yacht. Word is you're a splendid sailor."

"Leo again?" he asked. "I'll take you to the island, Clio. It might do you good to have me explain why Leo over time changed tack and became enthusiastic about the right kind of development. We had discussed Aquarius in the past, never in any combative way."

"I'm sure." Her tone was conciliatory. "I didn't know Aquarius had come under discussion. Leo never said."

"Which is a great pity. Now, would you like a drink?" He stood up. "I have a perfectly chilled Dom Perignon."

She sank back against the sofa. "Lovely! Where *is* all the food?"

"Where else but the kitchen?" Josh called, returning a few moments later with two crystal flutes. He handed her one, raising his flute to her. "To a pleasant evening, princess." They went through the ritual of clinking glasses. He sat down again, outwardly totally composed, inwardly controlling all manner of rising emotions. "I don't like kitchen areas intruding into the living areas," he said on a level note, "however much they're designed to recede into the background."

"I agree. You really are an *amazing* man!" Clio sipped at her champagne. "This is perfect. May I look around?"

"That's why you're here."

Josh set off for the kitchen while she moved across the living room to admire a striking abstract painting, which had to be eight feet wide. She had no idea what it was meant to represent, but the Asian influence was in evidence, and a wonderful intermingling of colours highlighted by gold leaf that caught the eye. "Is that the *sole* purpose of your invitation?" she called. Surely that was provocative?

You want to provoke him.

"I'm not going to ravish you, Clio, as ravishing as you may look," he called back dryly. "By the way, I love you in orange. It casts a glow. But to reassure you, my job is to feed you, entertain you, escort you home. I have a limo lined up. I can't afford to lose my licence."

"Spoken like a law-abiding citizen. This abstract?" she queried. "It's wonderful. Owes a bit to Ian Fairweather?" Clio named one of Australia's greatest painters, born in Scotland. Fairweather arrived in Australia in his early forties after studying and travelling all over the world. In his final years he lived as a recluse in a hut he built on beautiful Bribie Island in Moreton Bay. These days she knew the island was connected to the mainland by bridge. "I can't see any signature."

"There isn't one. I never knew it—how could I?—but it seems I have an artistic bent. I wanted a big knockout painting for that wall. I couldn't find one that grabbed me so I painted my own. As you so cunningly detected, with Fairweather in mind. I couldn't do a *real* painting, of course. Just slapped paint around in homage to the great Fairweather."

"Were he still alive instead of long gone, I think he would have agreed to speak with you had he seen this. Maybe even given you a few lessons. *I* couldn't do this. Most people couldn't do this."

"I know."

It wasn't arrogance. It was a plain statement of fact. Where had this talent come from? It would be more than her life's worth to touch on the subject tonight, despite the fact she had spent a lot of time wondering who and what exactly Josh's father had been? "Did Leo ever see this painting?" she asked.

"Actually, he did, but it wasn't his cup of tea."

"Leo was a traditionalist," Clio said. "You're becoming quite a collector, aren't you?"

"Don't patronize me, Ms Templeton."

"What was I thinking? I meant your skill at choosing what is really *good* is well in evidence."

"You mean you grew up amid beautiful things. I grew up in pretty grim foster-homes and institutions?"

"There is that, Josh," she said gently. "But this apartment has great style."

All that abundant energy he possessed had to be channelled into all kinds of enterprises, she thought. "Do you need a hand?" she called. The most delicious aromas were wafting from the kitchen, redolent of the superb local seafood.

"No. Just give me another few minutes."

Clio was happy to. The experience of being here with him in his amazing apartment was far more intoxicating than any vintage Dom Perignon. She drifted out onto the spacious terrace, which was really a genuine patio, imaginatively lit. Beautiful big springy golden canes stood in tall, black ceramic planters, complemented by a fragrant line-up of flowering gardenia bushes in smaller matching pots. The outdoor furniture was black rattan. The custom-designed sofa could seat a dozen easily, upholstered in an expensive white fabric with black and white scatter cushions. A long, low occasional table separated the sofa from matching armchairs on the other side. Matching dining settings as well, one to seat eight, the other to seat four.

The smaller setting had been chosen for dinner. Just looking down at it gave her a rush of pleasure. He had gone to a lot of trouble. For *her*. The centrepiece was really lovely—three exquisite pink lotus flowers and their pods floating in a shallow-lipped glossy black bowl. The tablecloth and napkins were pristine white linen, a choice of sterling silver cutlery or black chopsticks tied together with fine twine featuring a small ceramic square with Chinese lettering on it. The pure white china was at the luxury end. Perfect attention to detail.

She was enormously impressed and suddenly realized that could be construed as patronizing as well. She had to be very careful not to gush with Josh, though she certainly felt like applauding him. It was clear Josh was one of those people who liked to get things *right*. It was part and parcel of the man.

"Aren't the stars beautiful tonight?" Clio exclaimed, gazing up at the great vault of the sky. The Milky Way was a broad river of sparkling diamonds. The Southern Cross, never brighter, hung over the tip of the complex roof. It was perfect to be here alone with Josh on such a glorious night. She hoped Josh was just as happy having her with him. Leo's death, great grief that it was, had nevertheless cancelled out all the restraints he had put on her. Josh seemed to be prowling around the idea as well.

Across the table Josh was thinking how beautiful she was with her charm, all her graceful little gestures and style of conversation. Once it would have been beyond all imagining to have her sitting here across the table from him. He had done everything in his power to become someone, to become successful, to *be* someone. He had always known at the back of his mind it was for Clio, the only woman in the world who he felt could ease the deep ache inside him and control the powerful tensions with her gentleness. He felt he had reached high ground just having her over for dinner, having her attention, having her wander about the apartment admiring things.

He had known nothing about music, literature, art, but he had learned, studying rigorously. Once Leo had got him started he had burned with ambition and he had lived up to Leo's very high expectations. Leo would not have approved of his granddaughter having dinner with him tonight.

Only Leo isn't around any more. High time you

recognized that and broke down those boundaries your old mentor set in place.

With any other woman he would have done so long before this. But Clio was very special to him. She always had been. He felt he had to approach her as one would a young goddess, with something like reverence. He had understood that from the moment she had kissed him on the cheek when she was nine years old.

Clio praised the various platters Josh brought to the table. She knew from her travels that most Asian cultures didn't serve entrées in the Western way. Josh had followed suit. "This all looks wonderful," she said with enthusiasm. "I wouldn't rate beside you as a cook."

"Possibly because you've never had to spend time in a kitchen," he suggested dryly.

"Well, there's that," she admitted. "You did this all yourself?"

"No professional chef hiding behind the scenes," he said. "My primary mode of action is *learning* how to do things. I'm no different from anyone else. I love food. Asian food in particular.

The way it's presented so beautifully. Just because I'm on my own, it doesn't mean I'll settle for fast food. I don't."

The freshly shucked oysters were superb, served with a spicy Asian version of the classic basil pesto. Clio could taste the chilli and the coriander. She took a small helping of the Vietnamese chicken and prawn salad sprinkled with ground roasted peanuts. *Delicious!* The same could be said of the salt and pepper baby squid with green papaya. A melt-in-the-mouth barramundi parcel with a ginger and spring-onion sauce arranged on bok choy and she thought she had never tasted a better meal. Both of them had been using chopsticks, Josh with more expertise, but she wasn't far behind.

Afterwards she wanted to help him clear the table, but he wouldn't hear of it. "Can I at least peer into the kitchen?" she asked.

"You can. I make a habit of cleaning up as I go so you won't find a mess."

She made a sound of amusement. "You don't really need a wife, Josh."

He turned back to face her. He was wearing

a blue-grey linen shirt that showed off the fine set of his shoulders, dark jeans, a silver-buckled belt slung around his narrow waist. "Remaining a bachelor may have saved me a great deal of trouble." He smiled.

She tilted her head to one side. "You're saying women are trouble?"

"I'm saying a woman can bring heaven or hell. There's an old saying that happiness is part angel and part debt collector."

For a moment she felt saddened. "We love for good or ill, Josh. We can't take out insurance. Losing my mother robbed my father of all capacity for happiness. He's as connected to her now as he was then."

"Obviously he feels very deeply. Your mother's death was a tragedy. Some people *can't* move on quickly, even though everyone around them wants them to make haste. He should never have married Keeley."

"No," she said quietly.

They were inside the kitchen with its beautiful timber cabinetry, black granite benchtops, with light bouncing off the stainless-steel appliances, everything with sleek lines. As he'd said, absolutely *no* mess.

"You don't have to tell me, but I have an idea Keeley pulled the pregnancy trick?" Josh put the last of the platters into the dishwasher. "Your father, an honourable man, would have made the instant decision to marry her."

Depressingly true. "All in the past, Josh."

"So we'll let it slide. Have you ever seen a clip of Bobby Kennedy's address to a very dangerous crowd in Indianapolis after the assassination of Martin Luther King?'

Tears sprang to her eyes. "As a matter of fact, several times. The wisdom of the greats can calm the souls of the most violent and uneducated of men. You're referring to the lines he quoted from Aeschylus?"

Josh nodded, unsurprised by her knowledge. "He who learns must suffer, and, even in our sleep, pain that cannot forget falls drop by drop upon the heart, and in our own despair, against our will, comes wisdom to us by the awful grace of God." Kennedy had suffered the loss of his brother. Everyone knew that. You could say that by the grace of God Kennedy brought that entire crowd under control quoting from a Greek dramatist who'd died some 500 years before Christ.

She felt intensely moved. "Have *you* learned through suffering, Josh?" she asked very gently.

There was a faint tremor in his hand. He was *right* to worship Clio. "I've still got a way to go," he said, more brusquely than he intended. "*I* learned through books."

"Words are the physicians of the mind diseased. Aeschylus again."

He nodded, enjoying their rapport. "I read a lot of him. Leo let me take anything I wanted from his library. Maybe your father can dive into it as well. He might learn happiness hasn't deserted him. There are still wonderful things to fill his life. He has you. He should be looking forward to grandchildren."

"You mean I should be spending more time looking for a husband?" She stared into his beautiful eyes, received an enigmatic smile in return.

He recognized with searing clarity his own hopes, dreams. Dreams of Clio. "God knows, you don't have to go looking." His tone was tense.

"You want children, don't you, Clio?" His eyes traced the lovely sweet curves of her mouth.

"Do *you*?"

He was in no hurry to answer. "Sometimes I think I'd make a good father. But being a parent is an enormous responsibility. I couldn't live with falling down on the job." Abruptly he changed the subject. "Let's go back into the living room, shall we?" She was standing so close to him the smallest movement would be his undoing. What was so easy with another woman was difficult with Clio. The long years of conditioning had a lingering effect. He was determined he was going to do this evening by the book, even though his willpower, so dramatically forged, had never seemed so frail.

She's irresistible. She takes your breath away.

It was bliss to be alone with her. Nothing had ever felt like this. He thought he could move the earth for her. At the same time he was very much aware of the position Clio was in. She loved her father. Her father was his declared enemy. It could tear Clio apart to be forced to make a choice between them. For all the years they had known one another, they had only just arrived on this new footing. He would be wise to remember it.

Take it slowly.

His newly found material success would count for nothing with the Templetons. He would never fit Templeton requirements—lack of background, lack of family. What *was* known was his unmarried mother's drug-related death. Clio's family would not be comfortable with that. He didn't care a jot about them. Clio was his only concern. It almost made him want to go in search of the man who was his father.

They settled in the living room, their conversation moving at a leisurely, enjoyable pace over a range of topics. Their views were pretty much the same, even on the political situation. On the surface they couldn't have appeared more relaxed or comfortable with each other, but underneath ran a powerful current of sexual excitement that was hell bent on pulling them under. Josh's arms ached to pull her to him but he braced himself against the driving hunger to know her body.

Finally, when his inner conflicts drew to the force of a giant crashing wave, he straightened up, speaking in a tone that belied his true feelings. "Just tell me when you want me to call the limo."

Clio too sat straight from where she had been comfortably settled on the sofa. "Why, is time up?" Her voice matched his in casualness yet she was losing the struggle to hold her own strong emotions at bay.

"Who knows when a king tide will sweep in?" Josh said enigmatically. All he could see was her beautiful face, her beautiful body. He wanted her so badly the very air was being forced out of his lungs.

She stared back at him, absorbing his comment. "It's important for you not to get dragged under, Josh?"

He had never felt so utterly exposed. "It's *you* I'm thinking about."

"You put such pressure on yourself, Josh." Her voice was unsteady with emotion. "You can never forget yourself completely. I understand where all your control is coming from. But why can't you follow your heart, Josh?"

"Don't tempt me, Clio." His strong hands clenched. "The realistic likelihood is it could all go wrong."

She didn't answer, which could have been an answer in itself.

"Then there's the possibility I could go way past what you want, Clio."

She had long been exposed to his powerfully erotic presence, yet she said, "You won't know until you *try*." With his eyes on her, her whole body was aquiver, surging towards him. Had she known some of the things Josh had suffered she would have been horrified, but as it was she needed him so badly her sense of frustration overrode all caution.

"Give it a little longer, Clio." His gleaming blond head was momentarily bowed.

He seemed to be in pain, but Clio couldn't right herself. "Hasn't it been years?" she cried. The enormous pleasure of the evening abruptly was turning to misery. "Is Leo still manipulating us from the grave?"

"Don't worry, Leo can't come back," he said grimly.

"How many women have slept here, Josh?" she asked abruptly, pride bringing her swiftly to her feet.

He looked directly up at her, seeing his own frustration naked in her beautiful face. "I don't invite women here, Clio."

"So it's *their* places, then?"

His wide shoulders hunched. "Stop it, Clio. I've had my share of affairs, but none that really mattered."

"Why confine yourself to *one* woman?" Her dark eyes flashed fire.

Josh released a harsh breath. "There's always been that part of me that is *yours*, Clio."

Despite such a momentous admission, he started to move away from her. Angered beyond belief, Clio went after him. "Josh, stand still."

He told himself to keep moving, call up the limo. "Clio, please stop this," he said.

Only she was behind him, laying her face against his back, winding her arms around him like tendrils he never wished to escape. "What is it you fear, Josh? What is it about *me*?"

He, of all people, was appallingly vulnerable to this woman. "If we make love, it will change our lives, Clio," he told her with great intensity. "It wouldn't be any passing affair. Not for me. But you might have regrets. It could endanger your relationship with your father, the entire Templeton clan."

"Oh, to hell with them!" she cried hotly.

"You don't *mean* that." He could feel the press of her small, perfect breasts against his back. He hungered to take the warm weight of them in his palms, catching the rose-pink nipples between thumb and finger, catching them gently with his teeth, encircling each sensitized berry with his hungry mouth. He wanted to touch her in places he had only dreamed of touching her. He wanted to make love to her so badly he was astounded he was maintaining any sort of control.

"You surely don't wish for things to remain the way they are, Josh?" she implored. "Or is this some kind of waiting game? Kisses, no sex?"

White-hot excitement was swamping him.

Didn't she know that? He found himself nearly shouting, "Clio, *let go!*"

He hadn't changed from when he'd been a boy, yelling at her to go away. In an instant she pulled away. "Take my word for it, I'll never bother you again," she said in a frozen voice.

"Is that a promise?" It was a comment, so extreme, so perverse it had to be a form of madness. He had spent so long obsessed about her, yet here he was holding her off. Memories of terrible loss haunted him down his days. He didn't think he could bear having Clio then losing her should she ultimately choose family over him. Surely this was something they had to work out?

"Call the car for me, please." Clio had her face averted. She forced herself to move towards the door.

"Clio, you're not crying?" Josh's handsome face contorted with pain. "Clio?" When she didn't respond, he reached for her, taking hold of a bare shoulder.

She whirled on him, her beauty at that moment breathtakingly dramatic. "What is this, Josh?

You wish me away, but maybe we can do it another time?"

He didn't know what frightened him most, creating a space between them or hauling her into his arms. There was such a roaring in his ears. "Clio, don't cry for me," he begged. "Don't *ever* cry for me."

She was aware of his fierce agitation, knowing she was the cause of it. "But I love you, Josh," she cried. "Love you. Don't you get it? Love you until the end of time. Sounds like a song, doesn't it? I think it is a song. I've loved you since I was nine years old. God, isn't that extravagant? I'm just so sorry you don't *want* to love me." Tears were coursing down her face now.

He stared down at her, blue eyes blazing like sapphires. She loved him! That heartfelt declaration detonated deep in the core of his being. He willed himself to believe it. *Clio loved him! Could it be true?* "But if you were me, Clio?" he asked, nearly incoherently. "Think about it. If you were me…" He broke off as if he didn't know what to say next.

"For God's sake, Josh," she cried out in intolerable frustration, "you're a man women dream about. You make it so impossibly hard for yourself. You make it so hard for me." She tried to pull away, only he held her powerfully in place. "If only you would speak to me, tell me about your past, your pain, all the abuses and humiliations you endured, the cause of your burning rage. Only then can I help you. It's up to you Josh."

"Do you think I don't know that? Miracle cures don't come overnight, Clio, if at all. Please don't leave when you're angry. I have problems, I admit."

"If only you'd speak to me," she implored.

"I can't do that, Clio," he said, looming over her. "Not yet, anyway. I have things inside me I need to resolve. The last thing I want is to sicken you with any of my disclosures. My problems are all my own. But please don't leave like this."

"I *am* leaving, you crazy, contrary man," Clio was startled by the force of her own anger. "I want to help you. You won't let me. Well, I've had it up to *here*!" She put up a hand to a point high above her head.

All of a sudden Josh was swept by unbear-
able tenderness. "Where?" he asked, putting up
his own hand. "Your tears scald my heart, Clio.
What I feel for you is a fever that never gives me
peace. You say you love me. Do you realize you
don't *know* me? You only *think* you love me. This
is the fear. I only have to speak and it mightn't
be so. The words would stick in my throat. You
shouldn't rush to get angry with me. Please try
to understand." He bent his head to kiss her forehead, but when she didn't offer resistance, with
a shudder his body took over from his mind.
He began to trail kisses down over her face, her
flushed cheeks, beneath her chin, coming back
to settle compulsively on her mouth. He longed
to be freed from his chains. Could Clio do it? It
was a huge ask. "I'd be happy to kiss you until the
end of time," he breathed into her open mouth.

She was drenched by the now-familiar excitement. Kisses were wonderful but she wanted him
to carry her to his bed.

Abruptly he threw up his blond head. "I want
you to understand my need to set limits with
you, Clio. Some part of me believes you may

need protection from me. Leo believed it. So does your father."

"Oh, Josh!" It was a heartfelt lament. "I trust you with my life. So Leo tried to brainwash us both?" She spoke the painful truth. "He did help you in so many ways. You're right, he was *afraid* of you, just like Dad. Afraid you might steal their little girl."

"Maybe they were right to feel afraid," he said sombrely. "Leo, as my trustee, had access to my files. I have been violent in the past, Clio. Violence had become part of my life."

"At the same time violence could have been your salvation. I'm certain you would have always acted in self-defence."

"Not always, Clio," he admitted. "It's a horrible thing to have to submit to injustice year after year. Child psychologists who didn't have a clue. After a while I just kept my mouth shut. No one really listened. They wrote me off."

"But you've challenged the past and won, Josh," she insisted, staring up into his face. "You must see that. Leo's not here any more to direct our lives."

"Clio, he wasn't going to do that for much longer. He knew that. So what would you have me do?" he cried, clearly tormented. "Unleash my desire for you? I'm certain you've never had a lover who has pushed you beyond your accepted limits. You still retain your air of innocence. For all I know, you could still be a virgin. The Clio Templeton I know, is a young woman known to never take risks, or lower her fastidious standards, yet you say you're prepared to do *both* with me?"

She could see he was clearly a man at war with himself. She couldn't force him to submit to her will. "Take me home, Josh," she said quietly. "We'll speak again."

CHAPTER SEVEN

CLIO knocked on the door of her father's large impressive office that held all the trappings of wealth and success. Huge plate-glass windows panned across a green canopy of trees to the turquoise blue of the Coral Sea. His desk, big enough for a small dinner party, was a piece of splendid craftsmanship, made of English oak with an inlaid green leather top, the perimeter tooled in gold. Inside the air-conditioned office it was blissfully cool, but outside heat bounced off the pavements. The day was overcast with a late afternoon thunderstorm predicted. They could look forward to plenty of storms from now on.

"You wanted to see me, Dad?" she asked, shutting the door carefully behind her.

Lyle extended his hand. "Sit down, Clio."

She had never heard him speak to her in precisely that manner. Judge of the High Court. His manner was that serious. "What's this about, Dad? If it's the Oceania take-over—"

Her father held up his hand to interrupt. "I always knew how clever you are, Clio. We really didn't give you a chance. I apologize for that. You're a far better lawyer than I am. Crowley, that old windbag, wasn't even in the same street. In so many ways I'm enormously proud of you."

"But? There is a but, Dad?" she prompted.

"Yes, there is. You're my daughter. My only child. I believe I have the right—"

Clio broke in, trying hard to hold onto her rising temper. "Hang on, don't talk *rights*, Dad. I'm twenty-four years old. I'm handling serious legal business. I have my own life, but I'll always listen to you as a caring parent. So what is it? If it's about Josh Hart again, this meeting is over." She raised her voice to press her point home.

"Bear with me, Clio." Lyle shook his head. "You won't accept I have a right. What about duty?"

"Ah, duty calls. Then you'd better explain. But I think I know where you're going with this. You have something else that is damning to tell me about Josh, is that it?"

Lyle looked down at his tidy desktop. "Clio, you don't know this man. You only think you do. Mind you, even I can see everything about him is compelling. He's extremely handsome, clever, well spoken, thanks to Leo, sending him to the right school, then on to university."

"Come to the point, Dad," Clio warned in a tight voice.

"You were at his apartment the other night?" Lyle said at last, watching his daughter react with horror.

"Are you having me *watched*, Dad?" It was like a knife turning in her heart.

"Not me." He shook his handsome head. "No, no. It was your stepmother. As an older and far more *experienced* woman, she can see you're terribly vulnerable to Hart."

Clio let out her breath in one angry rush. "Just how gullible are you, Dad? I thought you and Keeley were divorcing."

Lyle looked uncomfortable. "We are, of course.

But Keeley said she wanted to do me one last good turn."

"I've got to go." Clio sprang up so fast she nearly knocked over her chair. "You really should examine Keeley's motivation, Dad." She could have said a great deal more, but she didn't.

"Clio, I've come face to face with a young woman Hart assaulted some years back," Lyle forced himself up from his desk to say. "You've only got to look at him to realize he'd be a frightening man in a temper. No way could I have him turning his temper on my daughter. Leo would turn in his grave."

Clio felt the anger welling up inside her. "Leo can do somersaults for all I care." Her heart was a deadweight in her breast. "You saw this mystery woman in this office?"

"Of course not." Kyle waved a trembling hand, shocked to see his lovely, dutiful daughter turning genuinely formidable. "I met her one evening."

Clio spoke with as much compassion as anger. "Dad, Keeley is an inveterate liar."

Lyle resumed his black leather swivel armchair,

straightening what few papers were on his desk. "Her name is Philippa Jones. Flip, Flippa, something like that."

"And you believed her story?"

Lyle rocked back in his chair. "I have good instincts too, Clio. Maybe you should remember that."

"Not when your instincts are muddied by jealousy. I don't give a damn what this *Flippa* Jones was paid to say. *I* am totally convinced Josh would never lift a hand in violence against a woman. He might knock a few male heads together as required, but women and children for him would definitely be a protected species."

The rupture in their always harmonious relationship was upsetting Lyle greatly. He blamed Hart.

"Now I have work to do," Clio said, "so please excuse me."

Kyle stared at his daughter's slender back. "Why don't you acknowledge you're madly in love with him? That you wouldn't care what he'd done?" he cried, his face flushed.

It was a struggle for Clio to stay calm. "Josh

Hart as a child was badly wounded by life. He carries scars. You wouldn't have wanted to trade places with him, Dad. Josh is to be applauded, not condemned because he didn't come from a *good* family, like ours," she said with heavy sarcasm. "If you want to hold on to what *we* have, you'll lay off Josh. And to answer your question, I *do* love him. I've loved him for most of my life."

Venom burned in Lyle's eyes. "Don't be ridiculous. You were a child."

Clio gave a painful laugh. "It might surprise you to know that Josh is the one who's holding off. Leo did quite a job on him. Brutal, when you think about it."

Here father didn't respond. He remained at his desk, head in hands.

Lyle remained in town, having dinner with his friend Dr Tim Maxwell, best man at his wedding to Allegra. Tim was now a specialist physician at the hospital. It was a regular once-a-month thing. Lyle didn't want to go home anyway. He didn't think he could bear the sight of his soon-to-be ex-wife. Keeley had done much of her packing.

She intended to buy a luxury apartment on the Queensland Gold Coast. Plenty of millionaires there. He didn't have the slightest doubt Keeley would find yet another sucker. But had she lied about Philippa Jones? The young woman had presented as well brought up with a sad story to tell. Of course, everything could be *arranged*, providing you paid. The sad thing was he had *wanted* to believe Keeley. He wanted his daughter back.

He and Tim parted company around ten o'clock. Both of them had stuck to a little under a bottle of Shiraz between them with their peppered steaks and salads. He was turning onto the main road, intermittent wipers on against the light rain, when he spotted Josh Hart in his silver Porsche. It was hard to miss. He still didn't trust Hart. Probably never would. But he could maybe talk to him. Face him down. He had a daughter to protect. Clio mightn't listen but he wanted answers. It was high time he asserted himself.

Go after him, said the voice in his head.

Instead of turning towards home, Lyle pulled out onto the road in pursuit of Josh. There weren't many cars on the road. There were lights up ahead and they were ready to turn red so Hart would have to stop. He would be right behind him. Maybe nudge the Porsche's taillight so that Hart would get out of his car to remonstrate. Or Hart could take off and leave him behind. Either way, he wasn't going to let this dangerous young man get away.

All he wanted to do was *talk*. Surely a father was entitled to do everything in his power to protect his daughter. Allegra would have expected him to *act*.

Clio had found bringing home work was one solution to her problems. Work occupied at least some part of her troubled mind. She wasn't sleeping anywhere near as well as she used to but finally, around eleven o'clock, she closed the case file she was working on, leaning forward to turn off the lovely Art Nouveau desk light that had belonged to her mother. She continued to work in her own study. She didn't know if she would ever be able to use Leo's. Leo had loved her but he had also betrayed her in his own way. He had gone about shaping a motherless girl into the woman he had wanted her to become. Full realization felt very strange.

She was almost at the door when the phone on her desk rang, thoroughly startling her. Who would be ringing at this hour? Instantly her already jangling nerves were on edge.

"Clio Templeton." Her voice registered her unease.

It was her father's lifelong friend, Tim Maxwell, on the other end of the line. He sounded so distressed she had to calm him. While she remained silent he told her that her father had been involved in an accident near the Banksia Close estate. "They're doing an MRI to determine any back injuries."

Clio spun her armchair around and sank into it. "How bad is it, Tim? What do you know at this stage?"

"It's not dire, my dear. I should have said that at the outset. Lyle's not going to die. I was on the way home after our dinner together when I saw the ambulance and the fire engine going the other way, so I followed them in case there was something I could do. Also I had this bad feeling. Lyle seemed very upset this evening. Didn't say why and I didn't like to push him. It could have been very much worse, Clio. The car caught fire. Gasoline escaped from a ruptured fuel line apparently. Your father owes his life to Josh Hart. It was a godsend Hart was in the vicinity. He pulled your father clear before the car blew up. He's in the emergency room, having burns attended to."

"Burns?" Clio cried, before her voice cut out. She felt nauseated.

"Second degree, love," Tim reassured her. "But burns need instant attention to reduce the chance of infection or possible scarring."

Clio felt so completely off balance she wasn't even sure she could stand up. "I'll be there in ten minutes."

A few minutes later Clio was out on the road with fear keeping her company. She just knew there was a whole lot more to this. Her father and Josh on the road together at that time of night? Josh passed Banksia Close Estate on his way back to the apartment. Her father's house was in the *opposite* direction. Was it possible there had been some kind of altercation? Tim hadn't mentioned whiplash or neck injuries, which led her to believe it was Josh's Porsche that had been the car in front. It seemed incredible to even consider that her father might have tried to ram Josh? Did her father make the first move? Josh was in a totally different category from her father when it came to driving skills. Josh would have known how to take evasive action. But had he turned on her father given sufficient provocation?

No, no! Josh had *saved* him. Josh had been no risk to her father. It was her father who was the risk to Josh. She had seen the veins in her father's neck bulging when he denounced Josh. This was a no-win situation for her. Josh would look elsewhere and he wouldn't have to look far. Any number of young women would give their all to have Josh. Why continue to bother about someone as problematic as Clio Templeton?

When Clio got to the hospital she wasn't able to see her father, but she had the comfort of knowing he was in excellent hands. She had to wait outside the emergency room while Josh gave the police a statement. She just hoped it would hold up. The last thing anyone would want was a scandal. The police could well believe this hadn't been an accident. There had been no witnesses to the crash. Or no one had come forward so far. Tim had told her there were skid marks on the road where her father had left it. Of course there would be. But there were also skid marks on the *opposite* side of the road. Could they have been caused by the Porsche? It would be a simple matter for the police to confirm.

Ten minutes later Bart McMannus, senior police officer for the town, emerged from behind the curtain. He acknowledged her with a small salute, before saying he was very glad things had turned out so well, given the situation.

Given the situation?

Clio didn't wait for permission. She rushed to Josh's cubicle, pulling the curtain aside. The young doctor who was standing there gave Clio a startled nod, then prepared to walk out. A nurse stayed put, all but glaring at Clio, but the doctor gestured to her to follow him, leaving them alone.

"Josh, Josh!" Her eyes moved frantically over every visible inch of him. If anything had happened to Josh, her last hope for happiness would have run out.

"I'm doing fine," he said, calming her anxiety. "They've ruined my jeans. Designer label too. But don't let's dwell on that." His tanned left leg was bare from the knee down, the fabric having been cut away, and the lower section was covered by a sterile dressing.

"You're not in pain?" She couldn't wait for him to tell her what had happened at his own pace. She had to know *now*.

"Not to the point where I'm cracking up. It's okay, Clio, *really*."

She gave an odd laugh. "Not in my book. What happened? What did you tell the police?"

"Excuse me?" There was a decided pallor to his golden skin, but his eyes blazed.

"I just want you to explain it to me, Josh," she begged.

He gave her a long, considering look. "I intend to, but not here. Any news of your father?"

Clio swallowed. "He's having an MRI. Tim Maxwell thinks he's going to be okay."

"What more can you ask? Maxwell is a great bloke."

"He thinks well of *you*," Clio said. "From the skid marks on the road, the fact Dad was going the wrong way! I mean, what am I to make of it?"

"You're suspecting foul play already?" he mocked.

"Don't be silly. Bear with me, Josh."

"Clio, I never laid a finger on your father," he said wearily, "except to pull him out of a car that had caught fire and threatened to explode at any minute."

Momentarily she covered her eyes with her hands as though visualizing a great fireball. "You could have been killed. Both of you."

"I guess you could say that. Goodnight, nurse! So what's next?"

She stared at him, hoping she wasn't making a mess of this. "I don't know what you mean, Josh."

"What is it with people who hate you like they need to?" He searched her beautiful drowning eyes.

"Dad needs help," she said.

"You're right. There's not a guy alive who's good enough for you, Clio. What your father did tonight was incredibly reckless. Is he quite sane?"

Clio sank down on the only hard chair. "Are any of us?"

Josh laugh came from deep in his chest. "Well, I'm ninety percent sure. I told McMannus I'd spoken to your father about the Aquarius development some weeks earlier. Leo's death threw us all. He didn't have a chance to get back to me. Your father spotted my car and decided to have a word with me right there and then. What really happened was that he was so keen to get it on, he nudged my rear bumper just to get my attention. I'm not into road rage so I took off. Your father followed. He's a lousy driver. He lost control of the wheel. It would have been end of story only a merciful God put me at the scene. How does that go down?"

Her dark eyes were huge in her pale face. "As a heap of trouble. What did Bart say?"

"I think noncommittal might cover it. But I'm sure he'll pop around and see me again. After all, your dad put about the rumour I was somehow responsible for Leo's heart attack. Isn't there a commandment that says you can't bear false witness?" he asked sardonically.

"Number 8. Bart wouldn't have believed it for a moment. I'm so sorry, Josh."

"Handy to be a Templeton, isn't it?' he offered dryly. Josh shook his blond head, remembering those moments when he had battled the dead-weight of Lyle up the embankment, wondering at every step if they would be overtaken by the blast. "You know, I could do with a cup of tea and I hate tea. Plenty of sugar."

"I'll see to it." Clio jumped up, grateful to be doing anything for him. "You *will* stay with me, Josh?"

Josh looked up at her lovely, pleading face. "I think I've earned the right," he said.

As it turned out, Lyle rallied quickly. The night that could have ended in horror and tragedy had been averted in the first instance by the tank-like construction of his car with it brilliant safety features, which nevertheless had not prevented a fuel line rupturing, then the incredible circumstance of Joshua Hart braving great danger to save his life. Lyle remained three days in hospital until his vital signs stabilized. No Keeley to sit at his bedside, quietly stroking his hand. Once she had ascertained with an old-fashioned phone call that all was well, Keeley had taken off for a good time in Sydney.

In the following days Josh didn't budge from his story. It had been an accident. There had been a late afternoon shower. They were coming into the Wet season with plenty of tropical storms ahead. Lyle wasn't the best of drivers. Understandably he was under a lot of stress following the death of his father. Alcohol wasn't involved. Lyle was under the limit, fit to drive. In his efforts to catch up with Josh for a conversation that had been deferred, he had momentarily lost control of the wheel, left the rain-slicked road and ploughed down the bank into a tree. Such things happened. The car was a write-off.

Alls well that ends well.

That was the word anyway. Bart McMannus

turned his attention back to solving who had broken into the Hudson-Smyth luxury home when they were away in Phuket.

Clio insisted her father recuperate at the house, where Meg could look after him when she was at work. Although she and her father had got Josh's story down pat, Josh had made no attempt to call at the hospital to see her father, let alone pay a visit to the house. Josh had made a clean exit. Not that Clio blamed him. The so-called accident had clearly been her father's fault. Clio felt very bad about it. What was most amazing was that her father actually thought Josh would call in not only to check on his progress but to allow him the opportunity to thank Josh for saving his life. Clio had to fight the urge to ask her father if he had gone to live in cloud-cuckoo-land. She was holding hard to the belief Josh simply needed a breathing space.

When Clio was leaving for the office that Friday morning, her father saw her off. "I really do regret the bad things I said about Josh."

"I should think so, Dad." Clio gave a short nod of her head.

"Oddly enough, my accident has given me a good shake-up in more ways than one. I'm even thinking about joining Tim and Anne on an upcoming trip to Auckland. It's to celebrate the big 5-0 of an old university friend, Louise Cartwright."

"Good idea. Go to Auckland, Dad. Enjoy yourself. Josh won't come here. We're not his favourite people at the moment."

Midmorning, unable to bring her usual strong focus to bear on her work, she decided to track Josh down. Her father might have been feeling a lightening of the load, but she was feeling destabilized. It was as though with Josh she had taken a quantum leap only to find herself falling back into limbo.

She rang his office, only to be told Mr Hart was out at the Sandalwood Estate. Clio rose from her desk at once. He wasn't about to come to her. She would go to him. What man needed chaos in his life when he could have peace? Josh could have decided he was well out of Templeton affairs.

Twenty minutes later she was turning into the Sandalwood Estate. Josh had much to be proud of, she thought. The development had a parklike setting with beautiful mature trees left in place and lots of green spaces. Kerbing and channelling had been completed. There was streetlighting overhead. People would enjoy living here. A dozen houses were already completed, at least four more under construction. She had only just pulled up when a workman in a hard hat came towards her.

"Good morning, can I help you?" The foreman thought he had never seen a more beautiful young woman in his life.

"I'm hoping you can. Clio Templeton." She dazzled him with a smile. "I'd like to speak to Mr Hart if I could. His office told me he was here."

"Sure is, Ms Templeton." The name Templeton pealed good and loud. "I could take you there, only look—there he is." He pointed to a sage-coloured house with white trim two doors across and down. "Josh is one developer who involves himself in every step of the project. He keeps us all up to the mark, especially when he offers incentives," he added with a grin.

"The entire project looks very attractive," Clio commented with obvious approval. "People with children will love living here with all the green spaces."

"Plans for that too, ma'am." The foreman saluted, taking his leave.

Clio began her move to cross the street. She was so uptight she felt more like she was swimming against a tide than walking towards him.

The sight of her rocked Josh's heart. Pure elation. It had been a shockingly painful business keeping his distance. He knew Clio had insisted her father stay at the house until he was feeling better. He understood that. She was a loving daughter. But with Lyle Templeton at the house, *he* was barred from it.

"Hello, Josh," she said quietly as they met.

"Hi!" She was wearing one of her sophisticated little designer business suits. "How are you?" His voice was very measured and firm, despite having to fight the urge to pull her into his arms. They *ached* with the restraint.

"Missing you," she said, and felt like laughing at the understatement.

"Works both ways." His response was terse. "I didn't think I'd be welcome at the house and, quite frankly, I know I couldn't tolerate your father. Not at the moment."

His face in the sunlight was like a living sculpture, his fine-textured skin gleaming with the lightest sweat. She had a startling image of him naked in bed with her such was his sexual aura. "I understand that, Josh," she said, swallowing against a dry throat. "I'm sorry. You need your space."

He nodded assent. "I need to cool off, Clio. How is he anyway?"

She ran her hand around her nape. She was wearing her long hair coiled against the heat but little tendrils were breaking out. "He's making a good recovery. He wants the opportunity to thank you in person for having saved his life."

Josh resisted a jeer. "I would have done it for anyone, Clio."

A moan escaped her. "Oh, God, I should have asked you straight away. How's your leg?"

He glanced down. He was wearing a white cotton shirt with epaulettes and khaki cargo pants. "It's fine. I heal quickly. There'll be no scarring."

"I'm so glad," she breathed, nervous with him despite herself. "Believe it or not, the accident shook Dad up to the degree he's almost his old self again."

"And what self would that be?" Josh asked sardonically.

"Oh, God, Josh!" There was a flush of shame in her cheeks. "Dad is seriously shocked by the way he's been acting."

"Really!" He took her arm, leading her into the shade of a flowering poinciana. "Was he trying to run me off the road, *kill* me or what?"

"He was completely screwed up."

"You think that exonerates him?"

A fallen poinciana blossom brushed her cheek. "I beg your forgiveness, Josh, and I applaud your magnanimity. You could have pressed charges. McMannus had to let it all go.'

"When our cover story was a total nonsense." Josh gave a harsh laugh. "I would have pressed charges, Clio, if for you. There's not another person in the world I would have done it for. Your father is a rich man. Why doesn't he retire?"

Clio bit her lip. "He's too young to retire, Josh. He's only in his early fifties."

"I don't think he should be practising law, do you?" Josh stared down into her beautiful, distressed face.

"He'd like you to come to the house—"

Josh held up his hand. "No way, Clio. Not even for you."

"Okay," she sighed. "I accept that. But it's been hard not seeing you."

"Not nearly as hard as it's been for me." He was employing every ounce of his powerful self-control. It had been his shield for so long it was nearly impossible to put it down. He couldn't reach for her, as he desperately wanted to. He had to give her time. She had to realize her position. She had to know in choosing him over her father and her extended family she would be burning her bridges.

Clio looked around her. Respite from her strong emotions. What once had been a wilderness of bushland had been turned into a housing development that took full account of the environment. "You should be proud of what you're doing here, Josh," she said with unfeigned admiration. "Your foreman thinks the world of you."

"He's paid to think the world of me." His smile was sudden, fantastic.

She almost had to close her eyes. "Everyone despised Paddy Crowley as a developer," she pointed out. "By the way, Jimmy intends to take his mother with him to live in Brisbane."

"Good thinking," Josh commented dryly. "I just hope Jimmy's at home with a baseball bat in hand when his mother tells that brute of a husband she's leaving him for good."

"Vince Crowley knows he's under close scrutiny."

Josh gazed down at her, his expression concerned. What did Clio know about psychopaths? "He's dangerous, Clio," he warned. "Like all psychos. At the end of the day no one has control over them. Take it from me. I *know*. Then there's the Crowley family humiliation. Paddy is no longer the big man in town. He confidently expected to be with Leo gone."

"God bless the guy who put the skids under him," she said with feeling. "Wouldn't happen to be you, would it? By the way, do you know someone by the name of Philippa Jones?" She spoke in a matter-of-fact manner. "Goes by the nickname of Flippa?"

"God, is it important?" Josh asked with faint impatience. He didn't want to waste precious time with Clio talking about a total stranger. "Who is she, someone from Sea World?"

"She could be." Clio had no difficulty telling the lie. "Never mind."

"Don't know her. Sorry," Josh said. "Do you feel like a cup of coffee?"

It was an invitation she couldn't resist. "Oh, yes, please."

"Come on, then. We need to take your car. Mine's in for service."

She stopped short, an expression of dismay crossing her face. "Josh, the Porsche was damaged, of course. I am just so ashamed."

He laughed aloud. "And that really hurt, Clio. I love my car."

"I'll buy you another," she said. "I wish you loved *me*."

His eyes, blue as the blue in crackling flames, swept over her. "We have had our wild, glorious moments, haven't we?"

"You're a strange man," she said.

"Aren't I." All he knew was his desire for her.

"You are."

"But you want to be with me?"

"I do indeed. Sorry about that."

He gave her a straight look. "Clio, I've given you fair warning you of my flaws."

"Who hasn't got them?" she asked. "My father, who has enjoyed every privilege in life, tried to run you off the road at the very least. Whatever happened to you, Josh, and I hope one day you will tell me, you were the innocent victim. Dad was the transgressor."

He focused on some point over her head, relieved beyond words at the clear way she saw it. It was a liberation. "I have no intention of letting your father get away with another one of his crazy stunts, Clio."

She could see he was in deadly earnest. "Josh, there's absolutely no chance of that."

"Maybe you don't know your father as well as you think," he said as they moved on. "When is he going home, by the way?"

"In the next few days. He's been invited to a big birthday bash in Auckland at the weekend. It's for Louise Cartwright, the biographer. Tim and Anne Maxwell are going too. They were all at university together." She went to cross to the driver's side, but Josh said, "Give me the keys."

"I'll let you loan it if you like." Clio said very sweetly and sincerely, tossing the heavy keyring and watching him catch it neatly.

"Could I take it to a party tonight?" he asked, his eyes challenging her.

She didn't hesitate. "I suppose, if you like. *What* party?" That came out sharper than she'd intended.

"Just testing." He opened the passenger door for her. "I actually don't want to go to a party and *you* can't party at home."

Spot on there.

"For God's sake, I thought you had long legs." He groaned as he adjusted the driver's seat.

"Come on! You're six-three."

"I don't know if you remember back to the time when I took a Beemer for a spin?" He turned to her with a beautiful, uncomplicated smile.

It was wonderful to be able to smile back. "It belonged to the very posh Georgina Reed."

Josh laughed. "No damage done. Actually, she was very nice about it."

"I bet!" she returned dryly. "Just mind how you go *now*." Clio let her eyes rest on his profile, the perfect straight nose, the prominent cheekbones and sculpted chin. "Sure you won't come back to the house with me?"

He threw her a droll look. "No, no, a thousand times *no*, Clio. Please don't be pushy."

In town they had coffee and a sandwich. Neither of them wanted anything more. What they really wanted they got—to sit opposite each other in spite of a difficult situation that was conspiring to draw them apart. For Clio there was enormous pleasure and comfort in being with Josh. She felt complete. "Would you like to come up and see my office?" she asked, as they left the coffee shop.

"I would indeed, Ms Templeton. Could never have happened in the old days. But I suppose it can with your father away."

"Well, do you or don't you?" she asked.

"I did say yes," he pointed out suavely. "I hear Templetons is a far nicer place to work without the late unlamented Crowleys. New beginnings. At least, that's what they all say. You're loved by the staff, Clio."

She flashed him a look. "Give me a break, Josh."

Josh's appearance in the Templeton law offices caused a sensation, albeit a quiet one. They were all dying for Josh to go into Clio's office and shut the door, so excited comments could be exchanged.

"Wow, like cool! There's a hunk!" Ellie whispered in Peter's ear, her green eyes aglow. "I've never seen a more superior-looking guy in my life! Those magnetic eyes! Kind of a blond Mr Darcy, don't you think?"

She sounded so thoroughly intrigued that hope sprang anew in Peter. "Darcy? He's not a client, is he?"

"God, you're more ignorant than I thought." Ellie gave him an affectionate cuff. "Jane Austen, *Pride and Prejudice*, dumbbell!"

Peter took *dumbbell* in his stride. Ellie's form of affection. "I did see the television production, actually. Didn't that guy take a totally gratuitous dip in the pond?"

"Didn't he ever!" Ellie leered.

So that settled it. Ellie knew how to appreciate a terrific-looking guy when she saw one. That was great news. To date he'd been unsure of Ellie's exact sexual orientation. Now he *knew*. Hallelujah!

Thirty minutes later, Josh rose from his comfortable leather armchair. Even in that short time he had learned a great deal more about Templetons and its workings. It was a very special satisfaction Clio wanted him to know. "You have a lot of files on your desk." He had been eyeing the bundles for some time. "Are you able to get through this?"

"We have to take on more staff." Clio rose reluctantly. Josh, trained in the law, immediately grasped whatever she had to say. Oh, to have him on the team!

"Surely you could do with them now." He frowned. Clio had to be overworked. "You won't have a problem hiring more staff?"

"Henry Morgenstern has two excellent candidates lined up. They're happy to relocate. This is a glorious part of the world after all and they'll be given the opportunity to spread their wings. You might consider shifting your business to us?" She gave him a sparkling look.

He answered her directly. "The truth is, with the Crowleys and, forgive me, your father out of the way, Clio, I would seriously consider it. You impress me in more ways than one. As it is, your father is senior partner. No getting around that."

She sighed, frustrated again. "We'll see," she said.

Josh was moving to the door. She followed him

up, loving the shape of his neck, the set of his shoulders, the muscular elegance of his body. "When am I going to see you again?"

He spun so suddenly she gave a gasp. "Up to you." His strong hands reached for her, moving down along the slender length of her, her sides, her waist, her hips. "There's no simple answer for us, Clio, but I have to tell you, I *ache* for you."

"I *want* you to ache for me," she said. "I want you to feel the *pain*."

"Oh, I do." He held her hips harder, drawing her into him, blue eyes smouldering.

Excitement, a boundless yearning amounting to a fragile happiness took hold of Clio. Surely together they could work things out? She loved her father but she knew she would never give up Josh for him. For the first time she saw light at the end of the tunnel.

"One of these days…one of these days…Clio," Josh muttered, "the gates of heaven might open to me." He brought up his hands to cup her face, before lowering his head. He was unaware his eyes had closed in the expectation of ecstasy. The tip of his tongue flicked over her lovely mouth, tracing its shape and plush contours, while she stood there trembling in his embrace, her whole body aglow.

His kisses were maddeningly gentle, tender, though stars were bursting behind her eyes. His kisses deepened. She started to lose track of time and place. Outside the door was the real world. Inside was her universe. With Josh.

"I want to make love to you," he muttered, his eyes still tightly closed, his strong hands imperceptibly trembling with the force of his desire. His mouth drank hers like a pool of nectar, before making the slow journey to the base of her pulsing throat. "God, Clio! Stop me. I implore you."

"What if I don't want to?" She gave a convulsive little shudder, drawing his hands down over her throbbing breasts, feeling his long fingers spread out over the contours.

"Clio, you *have* to. Kissing you and all the world is lost, but I'm forced to remember there's an office full of people outside your door." Even so, he couldn't resist pushing her silk blouse aside, bending his head to the upper swell of her creamy breasts.

She looked down at his blond head, her lashes long and dark against her cheeks. Love for him was drawing her beyond herself. "I know you love me, Josh," she said softly. "I *feel* with all my being you love me."

He lifted his head, looked into her beautiful eyes. "A man can be damned for his desires, Clio."

"But I'd risk anything for you, Josh. Why can't you do the same for me?"

"Clio, I'd lay down my life for you, but I have to consider you may have ceased to *think*. You have your whole life in front of you. You talk about risk? I'd sell my soul to the devil for you, but it's not *me* who might suffer. Don't you see, I could alienate you from your entire family?'

"My life doesn't turn on my family," she retorted, suddenly resenting her grandfather's then her father's interference in her affairs. "If my father and my family aren't for you, then they're against me. I can't play this waiting game."

Josh put her determinedly from him. "Neither can I," he said.

CHAPTER EIGHT

LYLE TEMPLETON didn't call ahead. He knew the chances were good that Hart would be in his offices on the ground floor of a building he now owned and had totally renovated. One wouldn't know the place! At least the man had style. That very morning he had come to the conclusion that if Hart wouldn't pay him the courtesy of coming to the house so he could thank him properly for saving his life, then he wouldn't exactly *barge* in, but as Lyle Templeton he was certain he wouldn't be refused entry or turned away with having a word with Hart.

Clio had told him Hart had made a full recovery. Of course, he was young and as strong as a Mallee bull, and his burns were relatively minor. The body was truly amazing, the way it went about healing itself. He was still feeling shaken, but he was well able to drive and get about. He was off to Auckland at the weekend with Tim and Anne. He was looking forward to it, actually. He hadn't seen Louise in years but he had read all her splendidly researched biographies and always e-mailed his congratulations. But first he had to speak to Hart. The young man mightn't welcome him with open arms, but there shouldn't be any bother. Hart wouldn't be where he was today without the enormous help Leo had given him. He didn't want to have to remind him of that.

Danny Morrison, a top member of Josh's team, put his head around Josh's door, a sparkle in his eyes. "Someone to see you, Rocket Man."

Josh looked up. "I've told you not to call me that, Danny," he said mildly.

"I know you tell me all the time but it comes naturally. We all reckon no one has ever taken off like you. Anyway, a Mr Lyle Templeton is out in Reception. He's sure you would want to see him. Big question mark there?"

"Not at all, Danny. I'd be absolutely delighted," Josh responded suavely. "Tell Chelsea to show him through. No tea or coffee."

"Gotcha!"

Josh rose from his chair as receptionist Chelsea showed Templeton in, but he didn't extend his hand. "What can I do for you, Mr Templeton?" he said in a perfectly courteous voice. "Please sit down." He indicated the steel-framed leather chairs facing his desk.

"Thank you." Lyle took such a time to make his choice Josh thought he might have been considering dusting the chair off with his handkerchief. "You're on the way to full recovery?"

"I'm getting there." Templeton began to properly arrange his expensive clothes. "I'll come to the point, Hart. I invited you to the house. I wanted to thank you for saving my life, but Clio made it abundantly plain you weren't coming. Is that so?"

"It is indeed, Mr Templeton, bearing in mind you tried to injure me. You certainly injured my car."

"Well, I'm sorry about that," Lyle said stiffly, "but you'd be insured. I was only attempting to speak to you anyway."

"A very vigorous way to go about it," Josh

pointed out. "You could have died that night, and it would have been your own fault. But I accept your apology, Mr Templeton. For Clio's sake. If it had been Vince Crowley, for instance, I would have pressed charges, among other things."

Lyle gave a snort of disgust. "I take it you mean an act of violence? Violence doesn't impress me." Abruptly he stood up in a kind of affront, convinced he and Hart would always be on a collision course. "Well, I've done what I set out to do. I've extended my thanks."

"And very handsomely too." Josh rose to his feet. "I'd like you to know I intend to see a whole lot more of Clio." He suddenly realized that for all the concerns that had weighed him down, he was a far more civilized man than Lyle Templeton, who had enjoyed every advantage in life. It was an awakening of sorts.

Lyle tried to get a grip on himself, but failed. "I never could stand you," he spluttered, incapable of letting go of his resentments.

"So it seems." Josh gave a wry smile. "But Clio makes her own choices in life."

"It was a mistake, coming here," Lyle fumed, full of detestation for the whole situation.

Josh shook his head. "Not necessarily. We've cleared up one thing. You can't break up the special relationship Clio and I have. She's freed herself of the domination of the men of her family. Personally I don't think you deserved her."

Hot blood rose to Lyle's lean cheeks. "How dare you?" He had come to make peace of a sort but it was turning into rage.

"Oh, I dare," Josh said. "The only reason you and Leo got away with all this arrogance is because you've always been cushioned by money. For years you both made me feel like I was a nobody or could never belong."

"Well, you can't," Lyle burst out.

"You're telling me *you're* a better man?" Josh gave a grunt of contempt. "I might have had a tough start, but watch and see how I finish."

For so young a man to be cloaked in such authority! "You have secrets, Hart," Lyle accused. "Tell me about that other girl." This wasn't supposed to happen, but it was.

"What other girl?" Josh was now on alert.

"You know very well." Lyle pointed an accusing finger. "The one you were alleged to have beaten up."

There was an ear-ringing silence, like after a detonation. "You should go. *Now*, I'd suggest." Josh's voice was very clear and strong. "I've never in my life laid a harsh or callous hand on girl or woman. But *you* could be in harm's way."

Lyle felt a burning in his chest. He knew he had gone way too far. It was time to back up fast, although Hart hadn't moved an inch. "Philippa Jones." He threw the name over his shoulder as he hastened to the door. "Ring a bell?"

"Get out of here, Mr Templeton," Josh experienced a flash of rage, though his voice remained calm. "I have no idea what you're talking about."

"I suppose I could be wrong." Lyle Templeton shrugged, somehow realizing deep in his heart he *was* wrong. Very wrong.

"One last thing, Mr Templeton." Josh's anger was like a force field that surrounded his tall, powerful body. "Be very, very careful. My good name is important to me. I'm sure you passed this scurrilous allegation on to Clio."

Lyle stepped out into the corridor before answering. "My duty." There was satisfaction in knowing he had scored a direct hit. "Good day to you, Hart. I can find my own way out."

Josh awakened before dawn. He was on the island. He'd been dreaming of Clio. Nothing new about that. It hadn't been a good dream. Whenever he reached for her he came up against a glass wall. He had planned to bring her with him but as usual things had gone wrong. He was here to *think*. Plan a strategy for the future. No future without Clio and he had to take control. Lyle Templeton wasn't the only one who had received a good shake-up. So had he. His concept of himself in many respects had changed. He had fought his background relentlessly and won. Unlike Templeton, he had been forged out of steel. Since that day in his office he had been steadily undergoing a turnaround.

Aquarius was such a beautiful, peaceful place. The ideal place to think. He lay very quietly in the makeshift grass hut he had erected beneath a canopy of towering palms. Gradually the indigo night brightened into a pink-and-lemon-shot pearl grey. He hadn't slept this well for days. He knew he had to overcome the tremendous feeling of hurt—damn it, *betrayal*—that was trying to pull him down. He should have realized Clio wouldn't have introduced a strange woman's name into the conversation without a reason. Her father had passed on to her a trumped-up story, no doubt originating with the poisonous Keeley. But instead of Clio coming to him and asking him straight out about it, she had tried to catch him out.

Goes by the name of Flippa?

He had mixed with a lot of girls in his university days—quite a few had joked around, claiming to be in love with him—but he couldn't recall any Philippa. He would have remembered *Flippa*, he thought. The whole thing was a total fabrication, its cruel purpose to damage him in Clio's eyes.

You haven't lost her, have you? the calm voice of reason broke in. *There was no bitter indictment, no challenge. She says she loves you. For God's sake, believe it.*

Only Clio had gone so far as to seek an admission he might have known the young woman in question. What sort of a name was Philippa Jones anyway? Nice and anonymous. Was it wrong of him to as good as threaten to throw her father out of his office? That was bound to have upset Clio. He could scarcely believe her relationship to such a man. Templeton had made no real attempt to ease the situation. His supposed gratitude was feigned. The whole thing no more than a feel-good cynical exercise. On the plus side, it had helped him enormously. Set him free.

Breakfast was a couple of plump, scarlet-flushed Bowen mangoes. Seagulls with glittering black eyes were keeping a careful eye on him. They must have thought he was okay, because they didn't fly away. Other birds were in the air. It was alive with their shrieking—terns, noddies, gulls. Shearwaters, a distance out, were touching the crystal-clear water as they glided and banked near the gently rolling waves of the lagoon. A pair of white-breasted sea eagles with a wingspan of over six feet flapped and soared on their upswept wings. There was an extensive fringing reef on the south and east sides of the island with innumerable gorgeous species of coral. Naturalists would love it here. Amateur fishermen, owners of boats, line fishing, no nets, would be welcome to take their catches from the island's pristine waters. Then there would be the scuba divers, the reef walkers. A big feature would be the observatory. He had great plans. He wanted Clio to share them.

What he had to straighten out was whether Clio had some lingering doubts. If she did, that would cut him to the quick. There was a soothing calm in this world of dazzling blueness. The strand-line vegetation, grasses and creepers, were a bright green, the coarse grass studded with hundreds of tiny yellow succulent flowers. Casuarinas, the primary colonizers, lined the strand. Pandanus trees grew further back, laden with segmented orange fruit. He looked towards the water only twenty feet away. The brilliant sunlight was causing quicksilver needles and points of light to bounce off the densely blue surface.

He'd take a leisurely swim in the beautiful

lagoon, then return to the mainland around mid-afternoon. Running his hand through his hair, he found a thick and unruly thatch full of salt. He had come over to the island in his racy little sailing yacht, Cuttaway. He loved sailing so much one might have thought it was in his blood. Clio would have visited the island many times with Leo. He had dearly wanted Clio to accompany him. Sad to say, her father's unscheduled visit had put paid to that. Could Templeton's detestation over time poison the situation between him and Clio? It all came down to whether Clio's love for him held up under pressure.

Josh had reached the apartment complex, ready to drive his Porsche, repaired to his complete satisfaction, down into the residents' underground parking area when a familiar figure rose up from the kerb and began to run towards the car, flagging him down with a wild swing of his arms.

Jimmy Crowley.

Instantly Josh felt the weight of worry drop onto his shoulders. He changed direction, drove ahead, pulling into the kerb but keeping the engine running. Obviously something was seriously amiss.

Jimmy was already opening the passenger door, a bruised and battered sorry sight.

"For God's sake, Jimmy, what's happened to you?" Crowley had obviously been in a fight and come off the loser.

"Time to go, Josh," Jimmy jumped into the car. "My dad has really blown it this time," he said. His right eye was streaming. His left eye was red and swollen, soon to turn black. "He started hitting Mum. He's just got to rage at her. Why is that, do you know? For once I acted like a man. Not that it did me any good. I should have taken up boxing, like you, years ago. Dad is beside himself with fury. Mum is determined to leave him. He blames Clio for Mum wanting to get a divorce."

"So spit it out, Jimmy." Josh spoke harshly. "Where the hell are we going? Your place, what?"

"No, no." Jimmy tried to shake his pounding head, stopped with a gut-wrenching groan. "Dad has taken my car—well, his car actually—and driven over to the Templetons'. He had a lot of nasty things to say about Clio. He reckons he's going to have it out with her. Called her a rich, interfering bitch."

"So the Templetons' it is," Josh said, very grimly, driving out onto the main road. There he put in a call to the 24/7 security firm, identifying himself then asking them to deactivate the system at the Templeton place. He had good reason to believe someone wanting to cause trouble had headed that way. He wanted access to the premises without setting off any alarm. He requested back-up.

It was Meg who had let Vince Crowley into the grounds. So trusting! She saw Jimmy's ostentatious car, and thought it was him. Precisely Vince's strategy. He was certain *he* would never have been admitted otherwise. Meg greeted his arrival with horror but he pushed her aside roughly. "Go get Ms Templeton," he ordered, tight-lipped with arrogance. "Go on woman. I'm not about to eat you."

"You'd need to eat me to get to Clio," Meg said, stoutly holding her ground.

It was then Clio walked from the living room into the huge entrance hall, alerted by the raised voices. Immediately she sized up the situation, pretending a confidence she didn't feel. Calm was called for. Not a show of panic. "It's okay, Meg." Her voice betrayed no trace of shock or fear, though the tiny hairs at her nape and on her arms were standing up. Vince looked frightening. He was a big man, and exuded anger. "What is it you want, Vince?"

"A few minutes of your precious time," he grated. "Tell your housekeeper to go away. There's no problem here. And don't bother giving her a look to ring the police. I wouldn't advise that."

Clio nodded at Meg then gestured Vince into the living room. Surely Meg would have the sense to press a panic button if help was needed. God knew, they were all over the house. "This is about Susan, I take it?"

"That it is," he agreed harshly.

Meg, who was holding a golf iron at the time, spotted from the library window Josh's Porsche driving into the grounds. She near fainted with relief. Josh would take care of this. She had immense confidence in him. She had discovered to her horror that the expensive security system was malfunctioning, or maybe she was pressing the wrong buttons. She was an idiot when it came to technology. To make matters worse, it was Sunday and Tom was out fishing with his mates. She and Clio were quite alone. But there were supposed to be many barriers.

Very quietly Meg crept along the hall and opened the front door. Josh was striding at speed, tall and formidable, Jimmy Crowley stumbling very cautiously behind. Poor old Jimmy! Meg understood Jimmy and his mother must have had a tough time. For most of her marriage Susan would have held to the fiction underneath the bad things that were happening that her husband really loved her. She had confided in no one. Probably she believed it was all *her* fault. But what about the boy, Jimmy? Wasn't it Susan Crowley's role as a mother to protect her son? It was all too much for Meg.

Josh signalled to her that he wasn't going in the

front door. She watched him very purposefully round the side of the house. He knew the mansion as well as anyone.

He moved swiftly, staying low. The house seemed deathly quiet. No voices issued from any room. Where were they? He knew security would be here any minute, just as he knew every second counted. According to Jimmy, his father had been just one step away from going berserk. Crowley wasn't here to talk to Clio. He was there to *hurt* her. He'd spent half his lifetime hurting his own wife. Josh hadn't the slightest doubt he could overpower Crowley, but he wanted to be in the right position and have the element of surprise.

The kitchen door was open. He moved through the large room equipped for a top chef then out into the corridor, pausing to listen.

Now he could hear voices. Clio's. An almighty wave of relief swept through him. She didn't sound the least bit intimidated. That was Clio. She was Leo's granddaughter after all. Plenty of guts. Then came Crowley's florid bluster. "I've tried hard to keep my marriage going." He spoke as if he were the partner who had been regularly brutalized. "What would you know about that, you smug, over-protected bitch?"

Clio's voice remained clear and firm. "Your wife lived in constant fear. Jimmy too. You would have made sure the worst injuries weren't visible so people couldn't condemn you. But they *will*. You're a coward and a bully. Don't imagine help isn't arriving as we speak. I will *not* tolerate you trying to intimidate me. You got in here under false pretences. Meg wouldn't have let you in otherwise."

"I was driving that idiot son of mine's car." Crowley's voice was a weird combination of triumph and contempt. "Fooled the old bag easily." He smirked.

"Well, you've gained nothing by coming here," Clio said in a clipped voice. "Rather the reverse. I suggest you leave before help arrives."

"I'm not moving, sweetheart." Vince's bitter voice curdled in his throat. "You think you can destroy my life? Get me tossed out of the firm? Make a laughing stock of me and my dad? Talk my half-witted wife into divorcing me? You have to pay. *You're* the catalyst! *You!*" The glare was one of pure challenge.

Clio came swiftly to her feet, recognising the blind fury. "You've lost your mind. Get out. I've already given you too much time. Your *wife* made the decision to leave you, even if she made it too late. I had little to do with it."

"Liar!" Crowley roared. The word pelted like a rock from his mouth as he sank into a pit of unstoppable rage.

He was going to attack her. She knew it. But that would only be the start. She could see the madness building in him. Clio flinched to the side while her body snapped into action. She had to defend herself. All along she had kept her eye on the small bronze statue of a young ballerina nearby. That should knock him out. If only she could beat him to it. She was prepared to make the supreme effort.

Where was Josh? she agonized, a prayer fluttering on her lips. Where was he when she needed him? Josh should have been here, only her father had caused more trouble, though he had vehemently denied it. Josh hadn't been answering her phone calls. There was a reason. Josh would have saved her from this monster. She felt like screaming his name. Josh wouldn't let Crowley get away with this. Hateful, disgusting man!

Josh...Josh...

However distant, her voice would search him out. She was sure of it. The bond they had struck was too strong to be broken. Josh would come for her. Only would it be too late?

For a brief moment Clio thought she was going mad. Even Crowley froze on the spot, his striking arm upraised. She could have sworn she heard Josh's voice. Slow motion turned to high speed. Josh rocketed from somewhere behind her.

Salvation! Her heart leapt in her breast. It was the *real* Josh, not a figment of her imagination. He stormed past her, launching himself at Vince with a thundering voice of wrath.

"You sorry excuse for a human being!" For a split second Josh paused to balance himself, then his fists shot out in a dizzyingly fast flurry of punches. Vince Crowley, a big man, didn't have the skill to block them.

Clio watched Crowley go down on his knees,

before landing face down on the carpet. Josh stood over him, looking very much like he was waiting for Crowley to get up so he could finish him off. She remembered now Josh had won boxing tournaments in his university days. He still kept in training at the local gym.

"Josh, leave him." Clio dashed the tears of utter relief from her eyes. She rushed to his side, getting a grip on his bronzed arm. "Leave him," she begged urgently. "He's not worth it." She could feel the tremendous tension in Josh's powerful body. Here was another serious moment to be averted.

"I don't know that I agree with you," he grated. "He needs to take a real beating to know how it feels. I didn't hit him half hard enough."

She tried to increase the pressure on his arm. "Josh, he's down for the count. There's no need to go any further. I don't *want* you to go any further."

He swung his blond head in agitation. His hair was so thickly tousled it was forming deep waves and springing curls. He stared at her with such a blaze in his eyes. "Clio, if I hadn't arrived he would have *assaulted* you." He spoke as though he wasn't at all sure she realized that. "He could have *killed* you. It wouldn't have taken much. A woman is an easy target. This guy is capable of murder."

Clio didn't doubt it. "Josh I understand that." She held his burning gaze. "But you must let the police handle it. I don't want *you* involved in any trouble."

Josh's handsome face was drawn incredibly taut, indicating the high level of emotion inside him. "I dare say his wife and kid hit the ground many a time." There was a dangerous edge to his voice. "Crowley, the big man! The street good guy, the home monster. How do they get away with it? She could have gone to the police. Maybe she would have had he ruined her face. As for poor Jimmy!" He couldn't hide his pity. "It was Jimmy who was waiting for me. He led me here. So I guess he passed some sort of a test."

"Jimmy isn't *you*, Josh. Your early life would have killed him or set him on a self-destructive path."

"Poor old Jimmy!" Josh released a slow breath

of tension. "Look at this guy." Vince was conscious and moaning, with Josh's boot in the small of his back. "It's possible he'd like to see *me* charged for assault."

"Not if I have anything to do with it!" Meg's voice rang out. She rushed into the living room, still holding the golf iron.

Josh turned on her. "Meg, how could you have been so foolish as to let him in?"

"Wretched man! I thought it was Jimmy, you see. Jimmy's harmless. The security man is here, my dears, *and* Sergeant McMannus, thank God."

"Is he dead?" Meg asked, taking a speculative look at the man on the carpet.

"Dead men don't groan, Meg," Josh pointed out dryly as Crowley tried to speak. "Don't say a word, Vince," he warned.

"Let McMannus take care of it, Josh," Clio cautioned him again.

It seemed like an eternity before Josh nodded.

McMannus had taken charge. Vince Crowley was cuffed, read his rights. He was taken away, protesting at the top of his lungs they would all *pay*.

"Get Don Burchell down to the station, you idiot," he snarled over his shoulder at his son.

"Might take a bit of time, Dad," Jimmy called back. "Burchell is holidaying in Thailand."

"Use your head, then, you idiot. Get Stewart."

"Make the phone call yourself, Dad. I'm pressing charges. So is Mum. So is Clio."

"Traitor!" Crowley yelled.

"I'm sorry, Jimmy," Clio said, as they watched the police car move slowly down the drive towards the open front gates.

Jimmy actually smiled through his injuries. "No worries! This is absolutely the best it gets. Should have happened long ago."

"Maybe we should get you to a hospital?" Clio voiced her concern. Poor bruised and battered Jimmy was swaying on his feet.

"I'll take him." Josh moved to support the young man. "Come on, Jimmy. We'll swing by and pick up your mother."

Jimmy's swollen face lit up. "Oh, great!" he cried. "You're a top bloke, Josh. A real friend."

"Count on it," said Josh.

* * *

It was getting on towards dusk before Tom Palmer returned with his catch after a very re-warding day fishing the rich Coral Sea waters. Meg told him the whole story while Tom looked on with an expression of deep concern. "I often wondered about Crowley," he said. "You have to wonder why Mrs Crowley didn't step forward."

"He'd broken her spirit, Tom," Clio answered.

"You're not going to let it slide, are you, Clio? I mean the Crowleys and all? I couldn't count the number of times Crowley has been to the house."

"In Leo's day," Clio pointed out. "Not that Leo had any idea what kind of a monster Vince was at home. A browbeater, yes, physical abuse, no. I won't let it drop, Tom. Crowley can get much-needed therapy in prison."

Tom grinned. "I don't doubt he'll cop the odd punch from a person or persons unknown when they find out what he's in for."

"Serve him right!" said Meg. "I despise wife beaters."

Josh had told her he would come back. It was well after 7 p.m. and he still hadn't returned. She was feeling very jumpy. God knew what would have happened to her without Josh. Meg had gone off with her husband, looking thoroughly chastened. Clio felt she had to take some responsibility. Although she had explained a number of times to Meg how the security system worked, she knew Meg only listened with half an ear. It had taken Meg ages before she had mastered sending e-mails. She was glad her father was in New Zealand. He had rung her twice to say everything was going really well.

"Nothing like a reunion! Louise looks marvellous! Hasn't aged in twenty years. Good-looking woman that! We're all getting along as splendidly as we did in our student days."

Clio had understood from a few teasing remarks her mother had made from time to time that her father and Louise Cartwright might have enjoyed a brief affair. Louise had never married, perhaps concentrating on her career. Clio couldn't help hoping Louise and her father might pick up where they'd left off, because no one on earth had the power to separate her from Josh.

Josh arrived back less than half an hour later.

Clio greeted him anxiously at the door. "I was getting worried."

"No need." He didn't attempt to kiss her. Her heart sank. "But everything takes time. Susan and Jimmy received treatment at the hospital. I dropped them back home. Crowley is spending a night in the cells. Sunday, not a lawyer in sight. Isn't that great? Even Paddy didn't show up. Crowley will be held on remand until the case comes before the magistrate, probably at the end of next week. Give him time to think. Meanwhile, Susan and Jimmy will be taking sanctuary with Susan's sister in Sydney while they sort out their lives."

"What a scandal!" Clio said.

"I don't think anyone will be surprised."

"Is there something wrong, Josh?" She stared up into his give-nothing-away face.

"Why should there be?" He met her gaze. "Case close. Or almost."

"I'm talking about you and me. You're distressed about something. I can feel it. You haven't been in contact. It has nothing to do with the

Crowleys. There's something else hanging between us."

"And here I was thinking I had mastered inscrutable."

"Not from *me*."

"Seems not." He met her searching eyes.

"Are you okay?"

"Fine."

"You wouldn't let me beat him up, even though he was about to attack you."

"Only you were there," she said with a faint shudder.

"Thank God for that!" He spoke with great fervour, staring down at her.

"My hero!"

"I'd like to think I am."

She was wearing a turquoise tank top with a longish floral skirt that picked up the colour. The top was embroidered with gold sparkles around the oval neck. The silk clung to the small perfectly shaped mounds of her breasts. He wanted to reach out to her, smooth the shining length of her hair that had such a heavy silken look to it.

But he held off until he could get things straight. "Meg gone off?" he asked.

She nodded. "She was terribly upset with herself. The security system is beyond her. Technology is a foreign country and Meg can't speak a word."

"I can teach her," Josh said with easy confidence. "She has to put her mind to it. Not let it go in one ear and out the other. Could I get a sandwich and a cup of coffee?"

"Of course you can!" Her anxiety faded a little. "Come through to the kitchen."

"Sure you can handle it?"

"I won't deign to reply to that. I haven't had anything to eat myself. Didn't feel like it. There'll be plenty of food. Always is. Have you been over to the island?"

"How did you guess?"

She turned to face him. "Your tan is even deeper, and your hair is all tousled. I thought you wanted me to go with you?" She had dreamed of it. The two of them alone on a coral island.

"That was the plan, but something always gets in the way." Josh swept an uncaring hand over his springing blond hair. "Remember asking me if I knew a Philippa—Flippa Jones?" He gave her a very straight look.

The *one* thing she hadn't considered. "Oh, my God, so that's it!" Clio said with a wail. "Dad spoke to you about her?"

"I'm not interested in what your *dad* had to say, Clio."

"He shouldn't have said it." The faintest sob escaped her. "Sometimes my father is a complete mystery to me."

"He's a difficult man, but *you*, Clio! Why did you have to drop in that careless little question? *Do you happen to know anyone by the name of Philippa Jones?*" His tone mimicked hers exactly. "It seems to me I might never earn your total trust."

She felt a powerful wash of remorse. "Josh I regret more than I can say mentioning it to you."

"But you *did* say it, Clio. Nothing can change that."

He was looking at her so critically she burst out, "Why are you so judgmental? Haven't *you* made mistakes? Said things you later regretted?"

His burned gaze whipped over her. "Maybe I regret telling you how badly I want you." Out of nowhere his demons were suddenly let loose. "Maybe I regret having anything to do with you at all." He turned as though he intended leaving.

"Josh, you come back here," Clio cried. "Don't run away. That's not going to solve anything. If you care about me at all, and you *do*, you'll listen. Dad upset me terribly. Turn around, Josh." She prayed he would. He didn't. "It wasn't because I believed one word of what he was telling me, but the fact that he could say it at all. Keeley set it up. Dad is as gullible as they come. I believed in you, Josh. Don't hold one stupid mistake against me. You're the best man I've ever known."

"I'd better go while I still have strength," Josh rasped. "I need to cool down. I'll fix myself something at home."

"It's easier to go, isn't it?" she challenged, driven to running after him. Yet again. She who had never run after any man. "You turn my life upside down, this way, that—"

"Okay, so you know your compass." He turned,

speaking in a cool, satirical voice, but there was a fierce look in his eyes.

"Sarcasm noted, Josh. After all you do to me, for me, you think you can stalk off into the sunset. What makes you tick, Josh?" she cried, fire and sorrow in her eyes. "Have you been hurt so badly you can't let anyone into every corner of your heart? Or don't you have a heart? If saying something stupid is the *worst* thing I can do—"

"Stop it, Clio." His handsome face was taut. "Just stop it." He had to clench his hands to stop their trembling. He was aching, in pain, his jaw tense, as it always was when he was holding on tight. He knew if he touched her he would forget everything. He would pick her up in his arms and have her, the incredible sweetness and beauty of her. "Let me go home. We can talk again." His voice sounded agitated even to his own ears.

"I damned well won't let you go." Clio gripped his arm. "What are you trying to do?" She spoke in bewilderment, reacting to something she saw in the depths of his eyes. "Protect me in some strange way?"

He threw up his blond head. The gesture was so

imperious it had to be in his DNA. "I see it as my job to protect you, Clio. Even against yourself."

"You feel my love for you might falter if put to the test? You still feel Leo, your benefactor, would have been totally against us?"

"You know he would," he said bluntly.

"So you're going to punish us both because of Leo?" she asked in an impassioned voice.

"Forget Leo. But Leo was the Big Man, Clio. God knows what would have happened to me without his patronage."

"He made you pay, though, didn't he? He made us *both* pay. Leo was close to being the world's biggest snob. And on the basis of what? What did he have to be snobbish about anyway? Does having a great deal of money turn a man into a prince? I don't think so. *You* could be a prince for all we know. You certainly look like one."

"Oh, Clio, don't be ridiculous," he groaned. "Born a pauper."

"What's that got to do with it? Don't you ever feel you'd like to know who your father was?" She broached that fraught subject again, but with great urgency, wondering if she was a bit crazy to start this.

"I don't want to have this conversation, Clio," Josh told her with finality.

It was time to back off, but she persisted. "But *think*. Dwell on it if you have to. You know nothing about him. It's more than possible he may not have known about you. He could even have been killed. Accidents happen all the time. There were no photos? Nothing you were allowed to keep with you when they took you away?"

A darkly sardonic expression crossed his face. "A koala," he said. "Satisfied? My mother bought it for me when I was about three. I loved it. I took it with me everywhere. Slept with it. In the home I got into some furious fights holding onto it. I felt no pain even when I was taking one hell of a beating and they had to pull me off much older kids. But it was a point of honour, you see. My only link with my mother. I still have it, believe it or not. KoKo, the koala. He looks pretty terrible these days. Lost most of his fur. There's a dark part of my life I try to overcome, Clio, but it keeps popping up from time to time. That's memory for you."

"Oh, Josh!" Tears sprang into her lustrous eyes.

"I told you not to cry for me."

His expression tore the heart out of her. She could see beyond the big handsome man to the abandoned small boy. She moved into him, laying her head against his chest, hearing the steady thud of his heart. "Bad things have happened to you, Josh, but good things are going to happen to you from now on. I'll give you as much time as you want."

"You'll give *me* time?" Josh grasped a handful of her long hair, turning her face up to him, amazed how the sadness and feelings of disillusionment gave way to forgiveness. He had his demons, but Clio had the power to exorcize them. Her love had taken him captive, offered redemption. He had been so severe with himself, holding off even when she had allowed him the chance, and she thought he needed *time*?

"We're meant to be together, Josh." Her beautiful dark eyes caught the light. "I love you. Love never lets go. You remember your love for your mother? How do you know she's not watching you at this very minute, wondering what you're doing, trying to fend off a woman who loves you."

There was wild confusion yet enormous elation in ceding control. He simply couldn't control his feelings for Clio. Never would. He wanted her and he was going to have her. But he wanted to go slowly, gently. For her sake.

"How many lovers have you had?" he asked quietly.

"About ninety," she said without a moment's reflection.

"I'd say two. How would that be?"

"Well, I haven't gone down *your* road with dozens of affairs."

He shook his head. "I don't remember any dozens."

"I'll have to take your word for that."

"It was at university?" Josh was certain he was correct.

"No big deal," she sighed. "All my friends were in some kind of a relationship. It all comes down to *couples*, doesn't it, Josh? Singles are the odd ones out."

"You made your own choices?"

"Of course I did, Josh," she said with a tiny touch of heat. "I was treated with gentleness and respect. I went to Simon's wedding a year ago. Michael is happily engaged. We all talk to one another. What about you? Still talk to the old girlfriends?"

He gave a twisted smile. "They all went into the convent."

"Terrific, lives put on ice. What are you really getting at, Josh?"

"Simon and Michael would stop whenever you wanted?"

She stared up at him, wondering what he was getting at. "Josh, you think I can't do intense? I didn't fall apart when you kissed me, did I?'

"It was more *me* falling apart, Clio," he answered with grim humour. "I've had such a different life from you. I fear with *you* that my emotions might get out of hand. I mightn't even *hear* you if you cried for me to stop. Love can be very fierce, Clio, passionately erotic as well as tender. I want to burn into your beautiful body. I want to burn out the good respectful guys, burn your every memory of them. I do admit to a fear that what I feel for you will get the better of me. That might be difficult for you to understand."

There was no doubt he was still seeing himself through the eyes of his past. "I do understand it, Josh. I understand how our early environment shapes us. It's a tragedy you knew little of the warmth and affection, the friendships most of us take for granted. But there's so much strength in you. There's all the evidence to prove it. You saved my father, who has done everything in his power to make a strong case against you in this very town. You're a fine man. I'm the *woman* who loves you. Not a nine-year-old girl. Sometimes I think that image you have of me overtakes the reality. You break my heart. You're so frantic not to hurt me. But don't you realize that's an aspect that proves your love?" She picked up one of his hands and kissed it.

"Clio!" Every nerve ending in his body ignited.

"Come with me." Her voice was husky with emotion.

He made an instinctive movement to resist. "Josh, I insist!"

"Do you just?" He had never felt such liberation. He swooped her up, holding her without effort against his chest. "Insist is a pretty strong word."

She threw her arms around his neck, exulting in the fact they were at long last to come together. She was fully aware she was leaving behind the young woman she had been. She was turning over her body and soul to a man who in many ways would master her. Josh was no ordinary man. Her mind was clear on that. But she wasn't about to be outmatched. She wasn't so ordinary either. Her soul flew from her body, soared like a bird.

In the end she wanted everything he wanted. He didn't have to coax her. They were perfectly matched in their roles of lovers. Her body fitted his perfectly. She responded to every skilful caress of his hand as his hard-muscled body, tapering waist, sculpted hips, firm buttocks, long splendid legs did to hers. She had never known such pleasure of discovery. She could only marvel at it. He kissed her from the top of her forehead, right down her body, pausing at her breasts with their peaked nipples and finally reaching her arched insteps, holding her narrow feet in his hands.

Tears of rapture filled her eyes.

Josh moved back, held himself at arm's length from her body. "I love you. I adore you. There's no escape."

"You know you have to marry me?" she whispered.

"I'd do *anything* to keep you with me," he whispered back. He bent to kiss her, her mouth opening like a flower at the first entry of his tongue. "I'm not the easiest man in the world, Clio, but I swear I will protect you with my life." For the first time in his troubled existence he was ready to consider miracles.

"I'm your woman. You're my man," Clio said with great simplicity. "My perfect mate."

Josh was too overcome to speak. Slowly, he lowered his body over hers.

Two bodies fused. Became one. Two souls took flight as if they had wings.

EPILOGUE

WHEN Josh first showed his beautiful wife the only memento of his early childhood, the koala his mother had bought for him, Clio clutched the toy marsupial, light grey in colour with bright blue glass eyes, to her. Her eyes filled with tears. She took a gentle hold of the sparsely furred ears, then lowered her head to kiss the top of the toy koala's head. She felt unbearably touched.

"He's in a sorry state, isn't he?" Josh, who had never imagined such happiness as now existed in his life, smiled at her. "The fur used to be thick."

Clio was running her fingers lightly back and forth over the toy. She encountered a line of stitching under the chin. A repair? On closer examination she found the stitching, very fine and very tight, showed a slight gap. She put an exploratory finger into it, encountering a small hard object. "There's something in here, Josh."

"Are you serious?" His mouth quirked.

"I might tear the stitching a bit if I try to get it out. No, wait, I've got it."

"What is it?"

She gave him the strangest look, opening her hand.

"For God's sake!" Josh stared in shocked amazement at the man's heavy gold dress ring, medieval in style, Clio held balanced on her palm. "That's a ruby, isn't it? Couldn't be. It's too big."

"It's a ruby all right." Clio gave her informed opinion. "It would have to be at least 9 carats. Glorious colour. It's described as pigeon-blood red, the brightest and most valuable of all rubies. You would have to pay a fortune for this today— the size, the colour, the clarity."

"What's it doing inside poor old KoKo?" Josh asked, shooting her a glance. "Frankly, I'm amazed."

"It was a safe place when you think about it, stitched in very tight," Clio passed the ring to her husband. "No one would suspect something like what you've got in your hand would be sewn into a toy koala. Try it on, Josh. It has to be yours. Somehow it came into your mother's possession. She, most probably, was the one to stitch it in."

Josh made no move to slide the ring on his finger. He continued to sit, staring at it as if mesmerized. "You don't suppose KoKo has a criminal record?" He tried to joke when he couldn't believe his eyes.

"Try it on, Josh," she urged.

"Okay. It's not magic." Josh slid the ring down the third finger of his left hand. It was a perfect fit, the gold glinting, the ruby glowing against his dark golden skin.

"I'd call that magic." Clio pushed further into the cavity to see if there was anything else. "This has to be one of the best treasure hunts of all time." Mounting excitement was accompanied by a frisson of awareness. "No more wondrous precious jewellery," she announced. "A newspaper clipping folded small, a single colour photograph." Clio found her heart beating hard. "Oh, Josh, my love, do you want to take a look at this before I do?"

Josh appeared to be in a state of anguish. He

held up his hands as if to say, No, no! "*You* look, Clio."

"All right, my darling. I'm sure there's nothing here for us to fear. KoKo has held his secrets for over twenty years, but I fancy he's wanted to give them up for some time." She looked down at the photograph. It was of two young people smiling radiantly. They were sitting on a white sandy beach, seashells scattered around them. There was a stand of coconut palms behind them. The young man had the young woman locked within the cradle of his arms. She was very pretty with long dark hair and either green or brown eyes. There was no such doubt concerning the colour of the young man's eyes. They were a blazing *blue*. His hair was a windblown curly tousle of blonder-than-blond hair.

He could have been Josh.

Very slowly she turned the photograph over to the back.

Carl and me.

That was it. No date. No place. Just Carl and me. But the photo said it all. *We're so in love with one another.* Clio had a hunch it was a Top End beach, maybe Darwin.

Josh made no move to take the photograph from her. He just sat there watching her. Very carefully she opened out the old newspaper cutting. The article's headline was:

Piracy off Papua New Guinea.

Clio read quickly, aware that piracy had become an ever-increasing threat to shipping around the world. There was a photo of a small sailing yacht, Sigmunda, and the text reported the disappearance in the Bismarck Sea off Papua New Guinea of a young German tourist, a yachtsman, who had been single-handedly sailing around the world. His name was Carl Von Ritter, 24. It was thought Von Ritter had fallen victim to a pirate attack. There had been previous attacks in the area from bandits in little more than canoes fitted with bamboo riggers and a motor. The attack had come in dead calm conditions that would have made it impossible for the yacht to outrun the outrigger. A huge search was being made for the young man's body. Another search was under way to find and apprehend the villains, now suspected of murder. It was thought Von Ritter had put up a fight when the bandits had boarded, but had been overcome. His parents in Germany had been notified. They were expected to arrive in Australia within days.

Clio's throat was so tight she could barely speak. "Darling, you need to read this." She laid a gentle hand on her husband's knee. "We were destined to find it. It will make life complete."

Josh's expression was very intense. "It's already complete. I have you, Clio. You've brought all the love, joy, and fulfilment to my life." His loving hand encircled her neck.

She smiled at him with shining eyes. "But what we have now, my love, is the all elusive key. The key to unlock your past. The only answer has to be fate."

"So *tell* me!"

It almost sounded like he didn't want to know. "There's every possibility you can find your father's family, Josh," she began quietly. "That's if you want to. It's all here. I must warn you, my darling, it's a sad story. But in a strange way it can set you free, change your whole idea of the young man who I'm sure is your father. Look at the photograph first. Read the clipping. I'll go and tackle dinner." She stood up quickly to leave her husband alone with this momentous discovery.

That was the start of a reconciliation that was destined to become so much more. Two young lives had been tragically cut short but Clio, after only a short time, made the move to help her beloved husband find his family in Germany. All wounds healed, even the deepest. Josh wore his wedding ring on his left hand, his father's ring on his right.

Around the world the blood red of the precious stone, the ruby, is associated with feelings of love, of passion, of romance. Is it any wonder a young man would give into the keeping of the girl he loved a ring that was set with the glorious gemstone?

* * * * *

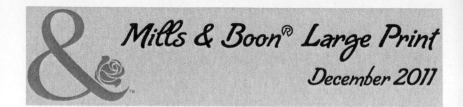

Mills & Boon® Large Print

December 2011

BRIDE FOR REAL
Lynne Graham

FROM DIRT TO DIAMONDS
Julia James

THE THORN IN HIS SIDE
Kim Lawrence

FIANCÉE FOR ONE NIGHT
Trish Morey

AUSTRALIA'S MAVERICK MILLIONAIRE
Margaret Way

RESCUED BY THE BROODING TYCOON
Lucy Gordon

SWEPT OFF HER STILETTOS
Fiona Harper

MR RIGHT THERE ALL ALONG
Jackie Braun

1111 Rom LP

Mills & Boon® Large Print
January 2012

THE KANELLIS SCANDAL
Michelle Reid

MONARCH OF THE SANDS
Sharon Kendrick

ONE NIGHT IN THE ORIENT
Robyn Donald

HIS POOR LITTLE RICH GIRL
Melanie Milburne

FROM DAREDEVIL TO DEVOTED DADDY
Barbara McMahon

LITTLE COWGIRL NEEDS A MUM
Patricia Thayer

TO WED A RANCHER
Myrna Mackenzie

THE SECRET PRINCESS
Jessica Hart

Mills & Boon® Online

Discover more romance at
www.millsandboon.co.uk

 FREE online reads

 Books up to one
month before shops

 Browse our books
before you buy

...and much more!

For exclusive competitions and instant updates:

 Like us on **facebook.com/romancehq**

 Follow us on **twitter.com/millsandboonuk**

 Join us on **community.millsandboon.co.uk**

Visit us Online | Sign up for our FREE eNewsletter at
www.millsandboon.co.uk